also by nathan englander

kaddish.com

kaddish.com

nathan englander

alfred a. knopf

new york · 2019

THIS IS A BORZOI BOOK
PUBLISHED BY ALFRED A. KNOPF

Copyright © 2019 by Nathan Englander

All rights reserved. Published in the United States by
Alfred A. Knopf, a division of Penguin Random House LLC,
New York, and distributed in Canada by Random House
of Canada, a division of Penguin Random House Canada
Limited, Toronto.

www.aaknopf.com

Knopf, Borzoi Books, and the colophon are registered
trademarks of Penguin Random House LLC.

Library of Congress Cataloging-in-Publication Data
Names: Englander, Nathan, author.
Title: kaddish.com / Nathan Englander.
Description: New York : Alfred A. Knopf, 2019.
Identifiers: LCCN 2018039092 (print) | LCCN 2018040330
(ebook) | ISBN 9781524732769 (Ebook) |
ISBN 9781524732752 (hardback) |
ISBN 9781524711573 (open market)
Subjects: | BISAC: FICTION / Literary. | FICTION /
Jewish. | FICTION / Family Life.
Classification: LCC PS3555.N424 (ebook) | LCC PS3555.N424
K33 2019 (print) | DDC 813/.54—dc23
LC record available at https://lccn.loc.gov/2018039092

Jacket design by Tyler Comrie

Manufactured in the United States of America

First Edition

For my sister

part one

I

MIRRORS COVERED AND FRONT DOOR AJAR, COLLAR torn and sporting a shadow of beard, Larry leans against the granite top of his sister's fancy kitchen island. He says, "Everyone's staring at me. All of your friends."

"That's what people do," Dina tells him. "They come, they say kind things, they feel uncomfortable, and they stare."

It's only hours after the funeral and, honestly, Larry hates himself for bringing it up. He really thought nothing could add to the despair of his father's loss. But this, this quiet, muttering stream of well-wishers has made it, for Larry, all the worse.

What he's taking issue with is the look that he's getting. It's not the usual pained nod one naturally offers. Larry's convinced there's a bite to it—condemning.

He doesn't know how he'll survive a week trapped in his sister's home, in his sister's community, when every time one of the visitors glances over, Larry feels himself appraised.

And so he keeps raising his hand to the top of his head, checking for the yarmulke, sitting there like a hubcap for all its emotional weight. Its absence at his own father's shivah would be the same as standing naked before them.

Sneaked off into the kitchen with his sister, their first moment alone, Larry unloads his complaints in a hiss.

"Tell them," he says, "to stop looking my way."

"At a condolence call? You want them not to look at the—" Dina pauses. "What are we, the condoled? The aggrieved?"

"We are the grievances."

"The mourners!" she says. "You want them not to show that they care?"

"I want them not to judge me just because I left their stupid world."

Dina laughs, her first since they put their father into the ground.

"This is so like you," his sister tells him. "To make it negative, to complicate what can't be any more simple. This bitterness in the face of what is pure niceness is on you."

"On me? Are you kidding? Are you really saying that— today?"

"You know that I am, little brother. I love you, Larry, but if you choose, even, yes, *today,* to throw one of your fits—"

"My fits!"

"Don't yell, Larry. People can hear."

"Fuck the people."

"Oh, that's nice."

"I mean it," Larry says, thinking that "fit" may not be a completely inappropriate word.

"Go on then. Curse at the terrible people who will cook for us, and feed us, and drive carpool for me all week, and make sure that we don't mourn alone. Yes, curse at the nice men who washed our father's body and prepared the shroud, and laid the shards atop his eyes, and now come to make a minyan in this house."

"Spare me, Dina. It's my mourning too, and I should get to feel at home, in your home, as much as them."

"Who's saying different? But you have to understand, they aren't used to it, Larry. Used to what you do." Dina takes a breath, reorganizing her thoughts. "Memphis Jews are even more conservative than the ones we grew up with. In Brooklyn, even the edgeless have an edge. Here, if you're going to be radical, people may, a little bit, stare."

Larry is now the one staring. He stands before his older sister, giving her the best of his blank looks. About what he was doing that anyone could think radical, Larry has no clue.

"Tell me you don't know," she says. "Honestly, tell me it's not on purpose. That you've actually forgotten so much."

"Honestly, honestly, I don't. I"—and here Larry was going to swear, which Orthodox Jews are forbidden to do. In deference not so much to his sister, but to the opportunity to prove his innocence (that he is not as odd a duck as they think him, that he isn't doing anything anyone could consider wrong), Larry rights his sentence and, with a stutter, ends it on the word "promise"—"I promise," he says.

"You really need me to tell you?"

"I do."

Dina rolls her eyes as she has since Larry was old enough to understand what it meant, and likely before. She explains what she's sure he knows and is—without a doubt—doing on purpose.

"You step out into the yard. You read a book," she says, with true sisterly fury. "You sit, like it's nothing, on a regular chair."

Larry straightens up at that, pushing with his hands against the counter, stepping back into the radius of his offense.

He gives himself a moment, letting the blood flow to his cheeks, his face reddening, as if, like a chameleon, he can change color at will.

"It's no reason to treat me like a freak," he says. "They're just stupid rules."

But even as he says it, rebellious little brother that he is, black sheep, and, yes, apostate, Larry understands that for Dina, they're much more than that.

For him to step out of the house. To read a page for pleasure. And, above all, to reject that special shivah perch—the low chair, the wooden box, a couch with the cushions removed. It is too much. That ancient pose, the mourner sitting slope shouldered, ashen faced, and close to the ground, it represents for Dina pure sorrow.

"A stupid chair isn't what makes it mourning," Larry says, doubling down.

Though he knows, for his sister, a chair absolutely did.

THERE LIES LARRY, WEDGED IN HIS NEPHEW'S NARROW BED, in his nephew's narrow room, freezing under a thin polyester comforter in Dina's arctically over-air-conditioned house.

Sleep does not come on the first night of mourning, when Larry, mustering all his Zazen-based mindfulness, cannot disengage from the shock of his own thoughts.

He wants to scream "Daddy." And he wants to scream "Mommy." And it's that pure regression, on top of the grief, that has him so alarmed. A grown man, frustrated with his frustration, wrestling to keep his hurt pent up.

If Larry wasn't already headed there on his own, Dina had nudged him the rest of the way back to childhood by sticking him in an eleven-year-old's lair, instead of settling her thirty-year-old brother in the more uncle-worthy den.

But the den is where their father had taken sick during his Passover visit. It's where he'd convalesced between the many trips to the hospital, until his final, fateful admittance. That room was blocked off in Dina's mind.

And so this skinny bed for Larry, on which he flips to face the glow of his nephew's aquarium.

Its watery light bathes him while illuminating the wall opposite, the fish gliding before a shelf of giant trophies, the likes of which Larry—in his sporting years—had never won.

And now he does not want to yell for his parents, but yell *at* his sister, furious over what, he couldn't exactly say. Maybe it's the light of the tank, turned blinding, keeping a sleepless man awake? Maybe it's because, in their already tiny family, his big sister hadn't been able to make their father not die? Or because, when he was his nephew's tender age, Dina, older, wiser, hadn't been able to stop their flaky mother from running off to Marin County with Dennis, her ridiculous, new-age husband—the newlyweds fresh from a marriage that took place the very day their dear father held the *get* in his hands.

Their mother had literally gone from her divorce in rabbinical court straight to a chuppah in Prospect Park. She'd forced Larry to hold one of the supporting poles, while Dennis broke the glass, stomping it with his fat, Birkenstocked foot.

Larry shakes his head at the memory, and, pressing a pillow over his face until he sees stars, he figures he's maybe mad at Dina simply for representing all that was left of the only family unit he'd ever known.

Now it was the two of them, alone.

Except Dina is not alone. She has her husband, and her three kids, and the hundreds of religious clanspeople who'd pour in all week. These southern, Memphis, Gracelandian Jews who'd never give up or go away.

Larry, overcome with exhaustion and emotion, with the endless exploration of his sorrows, gives up and crawls from bed. He yanks the fish tank's plug from the wall with a force edging on violence and sighs with relief as a restorative darkness floods the room.

Feeling his way back under the boy's blanket, tucking himself in, Larry floats toward sleep in that wonderful blackness.

But he can't let go, haunted as he is by thoughts of death and of dirt, of gravel thrumming against coffin, and the literal specter of a soul formally separated from its body—his father's ghost on the loose. With Larry's own body stretched out in that narrow casket of a bed and chock-full of superstition, it's as if he'd dug up his old religious self just as his father was buried.

Eyes closed, he tries again and again to let himself drift. But his ears train themselves on the fish in the tank, concerned with their well-being.

More and more, Larry worries that by pulling the plug, he'd turned off the whole contraption, that he'd somehow suffocate the fish, or undrown them, or whatever the term is for stopping things that breathe underwater from doing whatever it is that they do.

He can't, quite obviously, hear them swimming, so he instead tries to isolate the sound of the water filter—separating it from the unfamiliar electrical hum of the house. But everything is overpowered by the drone of whatever tireless compressor is anchored nearby, and forcing all that icy air through the vent above his bed.

So Larry opens his eyes again, stirring further, and strains his vision against the darkness, hoping to make out the smokestack of bubbles rising from that stupid aquarium's pump.

He is—and he knows it's not rational—fully terrified that the family will wake to another set of funerals, all of them his idiotic, avuncular fault. He pictures them all crunched into the bathroom in their funereal clothing, now poised over one of the house's stately, silent-flush, rich-person toilets. Larry's nephew will preside while his two nieces, like pallbearers, hold a fish-heavy skimmer, the kids watching those murdered charges tumble off to their maker, just as they had with their grandfather the morning before.

Every time sleep comes, the fish pull Larry back, until he drags himself from bed to plug the damn thing back in.

With the light burning, Larry gives himself over to the endlessness of the night, lying there missing his father—loving his father—who, white bearded and full of faith, had been the only one from Larry's old life, from their cloistered community, who saw his true nature, loving Larry for exactly who he was and cherishing the man he'd become.

"I want you to know," his father had said, from his hospital bed, "that you, in this world and the next, will be fine."

"You think?" Larry had said.

"Do you know what I think?"

"I'm asking."

"I think the World to Come is just a long table where every-one, on both sides, sits, men and women—"

"Pets?"

"No pets," his father said.

"None?"

"Fine," his father said. "Under the table, the dogs and cats. But no birds. I can't picture it with birds."

"Fair enough," Larry said.

"This long table, with its perfect white cloth, is set not with food and drink, but with the Torah, copies for everyone, so that you can read to yourself or learn in pairs."

"I can picture that."

"And you know what happens at this table?"

"What?"

"All you do for eternity is study. Nothing else. No interrup-tion. No day, no night, no weekend or holiday, no *y'mei chag* or *chol*. For it is the afterlife. Time unbroken—all of it given over to one purpose."

"Sure," Larry said.

"This is why, for the souls gathered, that single place serves as both Heaven and Hell."

Here his father had gulped at the air, fishlike himself.

"It goes like this," his father said. "If you have a good mind and a good heart, if you like to learn Torah and take interest in knowledge, then studying for eternity is, for you, Heaven."

He had looked to his son, and Larry had nodded.

"And if all you want is to waste time on *narishkeit* and bunk stuff, to think your greedy thoughts though the money is gone, and to think your dirty thoughts though your *schvontz* is buried down below, then for you that same table is torture. Then sitting there, with your bad brain, you find yourself in Hell."

Larry considered the idea, poised at his father's side.

Partly, he'd thought it was funny, and thought about making a Larry-like joke. But being his father's son, Larry also took it seriously. He was awed at the notion and somehow afraid.

His father, who could read him like no one else, reached out with his liver-spotted hand and, laying it atop Larry's, said, "I'm sure, in that place, for you, it would be Heaven."

Larry had gasped, not from surprise, but choking back the rush of comfort he took in his father's ruling.

"Trust me, Larry, it's all right that you don't believe. This period in your life—it feels like it's forever, but if you're lucky, life is long and each of these forevers will one day seem fleeting. You think when I was your age that I could have pictured this? That it would be 1999—the edge of a new millennium—and I'd be saying goodbye to a handsome, grown son at the end of my days? I can tell you that even back then, I already felt old and thought I knew it all." His father gave a weak squeeze to Larry's hand. "You're a good boy. And I pray that I don't see you across from me until you reach a hundred and twenty years. But for you, my boychick, when it's the right time to take your seat, that table will feel like a blessing without end."

II

THE SECOND DAY OF SHIVAH IS EVEN HARDER THAN THE first.

An olive branch offered to his sister, Larry spends the whole morning in the living room among the visitors, sitting on the appropriate backbreaking chair.

He lets himself be small-talked and well-wished, nodding politely in response to even the faintest of frowns. One after another, he receives the pathologically tone-deaf tales of everyone else's dead parents, the lives cut short and drawn-out passings, the goodbyes exchanged and the laments of those who'd missed the chance to lower eyelids that would forever stay shut.

Larry wants to say, in response, "Thanks for sharing, and fuck your dead dad."

Instead, he musters his own frowns, consoling in turn. He pats a leg and pats a back, and even dispenses one hug so fierce it sends both their yarmulkes tumbling to the ground.

Whenever Larry checks the clock, it appears to be frozen in place, if not ticking backwards. The relentless Tennessee sun cuts through the blinds, catching Larry in its glare no matter which way he turns.

Having squatted there cramped for as long as he humanly could, Larry hoists himself up and pads out onto the burning back patio in his socks. All eyes are upon him as he transgresses.

WHEN LARRY GETS HIS SISTER ALONE IN THE KITCHEN again, it's almost time for *Maariv* prayers. He goes to close the door behind them, when he hears the audible creek of a woman's knees from the adjoining room. It's one of the elderly synagogue members getting up to tend selflessly to their needs.

Larry pauses with that door in his hand and thinks at her, with all his might, "Give it a break, you kindly old bag."

The woman turns rigid under his gaze, before smoothing her skirt, as if that's why she'd stood. She then sits, slowly, back down.

Facing Dina, Larry can see that she's exhausted—not from hosting, or grieving, or parenting. His sister is worn out from him.

He waits for her expression to soften.

When it doesn't, and afraid of missing his window of privacy, he speaks.

"They hover," Larry says.

And what can Dina do in response but roll her eyes?

"Five more days of this," he says. "Endless days."

"Do you know what's endless, Larry? Do you know what—more than hovering—your sister can't bear for the rest of the week?"

Larry thinks about it. And Larry answers.

"Me?" is what he says.

"Correct. That is what I can't handle. What my husband can't handle. What my sweet children, I can already tell, will very soon cease to handle."

Larry starts to respond, but his sister, with a finger raised, puts a stop to that.

She is not done.

"Larry, listen to me. I can't keep reminding you that these are good people. I don't have it in me to explain, every two minutes, why kindness is only ever kind. If you want to see negative where it is purely positive—"

"Purely?" Larry says. "I'll admit, from people like this, at a time like this, there comes support. But that all of it," he says, signaling what lay beyond the kitchen walls, "is straight-up pure?"

Dina crosses her arms. Dina challenges him, silently, to go on.

"Pure would mean that they'd all still be here if you turned not-kosher, or anti-Israel. Or if you were suddenly gay."

"Why would I suddenly be gay?"

"Fine. Then Avi."

"Avi, my husband? Avi, who is horny even now—in the midst?"

"Gross," Larry says. Then, considering, "Sure. Gay-Avi. Would they be here in the same numbers if that was suddenly the case?"

It is a theoretical point.

Apparently, Dina isn't in the mood right then for the high-minded. And though she'd just yesterday told him not to raise his voice, she yells, pretty loudly, "Enough!"

The sound echoes.

They've heard it in both the living room and dining room, for sure. Larry can sense all those bored neighbors, poking about the table of bagels and cakes, with its too-many plates of crudités.

He knows they've stopped grazing at the outburst, that they stare through the wall, their chapped and cracking carrots suspended mid-dip over bowls of crusted hummus and baba ghanoush.

Larry takes a deep breath and tries to count to ten.

"Enough, what?" he says, way too long after Dina's yelled it. And for some reason he throws his shoulders back, proud, as if he's just delivered the smartest retort in the world.

"I have opened my door to you," Dina tells him. "My home. It's always been your home. And my community—it's always been yours too."

"What, the Memphis community? Where Elvis's body is buried down the street from our father's? Spare me."

"Memphis. Brooklyn. It doesn't matter. The Orthodox community, the Young Israel community, it's the same, anywhere in the world. It's your home, Larry—wherever you find it, whether you run away or not."

For her to say he'd run away, in Tennessee of all places. To say that to a lifelong New Yorker. That really had to top everything in this Grand Ole Opry, Gus's Fried Chicken, *Hee Haw* state. Where, if Larry wasn't already up all night because he was losing his mind, he'd stay awake anyway, afraid that a fucking fiddleback spider would bite him in his sleep and he'd open his eyes to his leg rotted off, if he woke up at all.

How could she, of all people, say he was the one who'd left?

As far as Larry was concerned, his sister had married Avi and followed him from Brooklyn to the moon. Larry was the one who'd put down roots in their hometown. Just look at his address. Wasn't the queen-size Posturepedic bed where Larry lay his head every night—in real blackout-curtain darkness—just three subway stops from where they grew up?

Wasn't the fact of his counting distance in subway stops proof enough? Could there be any greater sign of having remained within access to what they'd been raised to understand was civilization?

He is about to make this point. To dig into her, for real, when Rabbi Rye (of all the ridiculous rabbi names!) bursts in to drag Larry into the living room for evening prayers.

The wretchedness of the days is unbroken for Larry, but each is still punctuated with its own special torments. There were three occasions, morning, afternoon, and night, when the community made its minyan, and during which Larry was forced to recite—again and again—the Mourner's Kaddish.

Rabbi Rye convenes the quorum, and in front of all those gathered Larry worships with the *shuckling* seriousness and *kavanah* these professional Jews expect.

When the moment comes Larry calls out, so that they can respond to his Heavenly entreaties. He holds his tears before them and recites for his dear, dear father the Prayer for the Dead.

III

BACK IN BED, LARRY STARES AT THOSE FISH IN MISERY, trapped as he is with the single household pet in the whole of the universe that offers no comfort. He hadn't bothered fiddling with the light before lying down, resigned to perpetual sleeplessness.

What he had done, while the house was busy brushing teeth and putting on pajamas, was pull out his laptop and snake the boy's telephone line over to the night table where he'd set his computer. Larry poked around the Internet, squinting over at the tank, trying to identify what some of those individual creatures were called. He was hoping he might alienate a bit less and bond a bit more.

When his nephew came in to grab his stuff and to sprinkle food atop the water, Larry stood beside him and, pointing, tried to remember what he'd learned five minutes before. He'd said, "Is that a dragonet, the one behind those two?"

The boy—exactly as his mother would have—rolled his eyes.

"Those are all dragonets. The two in the front are red scooters, and the one behind it is a spotted mandarin. But all of them—"

"Are dragonets?"

"Yes," the boy said.

"And that little shark-looking one over there?"

"Is a shark," the boy said, shaking his head and leaving his uncle to his worries.

Larry now watches that mini-shark turn and cut his way, swimming to the glass.

He hugs the pillow to his chest and pulls his knees up, fetal. He thinks about how he'd loved his father. And how his father had loved him, had accepted him, and displayed—for a religious man—a different kind of faith. He'd believed in Larry's Larry-ness. He'd held sacred his son.

But part in parcel with his father's belief in him as a person, came a committed disbelief in all that Larry held true. From his deathbed, his father continued to make clear that the life Larry currently lived, that he'd worked so hard to build, that none of it was Larry's *real* life.

Even at thirty, as Larry's hair showed its first flecks of gray and the bags under his eyes began to puff out, the life he'd chosen was to his father temporary, a juncture that would end with Larry, as his father phrased it, "coming home."

Home.

To his father and his sister, home was not the singular place one hailed from. It was any outpost, anywhere on the planet, that held like-minded, kosher, *mikvah*-dipping, synagogue-attending, Israel-cheering, fellow tribespeople, who all felt, and believed, and did the very same things in the very same way—including taking mourning so seriously that they breathed up all the air in the room, suffocating the living, so that the survivors might truly end up one with the dead.

So much did Larry's father believe his son's whole existence was a phase, that during one of those farewell discussions, he'd said to Larry, "If you have any of those horrible hipster tattoos, I don't want to know. But I beg you, if you get any more, make sure they're hidden. When you return to the fold, it will be hard if you have some silly thing written across your knuckles, or a dragon up your arm. You will be forced to face such a mistake every morning as you wrap your tefillin around."

In that moment, Larry had felt a strange mix of emotions. He'd felt cared for. He'd felt hurt. He also found himself laughing. "Hipster," from his father's mouth! A million dollars he'd have bet that his father had never heard the word.

If they were on the subject of life decisions, it was as good a time as any to discuss the funeral, and the shipping of what would be the body back home to New York.

Larry couldn't leave it all to his sister. He needed, at some point, to grow up.

It was his father's turn to laugh, a raspy, dry-throated laugh.

No, he told his son. He wasn't headed back there. Not to Brooklyn.

The news hit Larry with a jolt. And then Larry's old head clicked in. Yes, of course, his father would want to be buried in Israel. When the Messiah comes and the dead are reawakened, his father wouldn't want to roll underground all the way to Jerusalem before he might rise. This is what Larry had been taught as a child, that it's those in the Holy Land who will stand right up from their graves. The other Jews will have to make the journey, rolling their jangly bones to the home-of-homes, before they might live again.

"Jerusalem," Larry said, nodding somberly and full of understanding.

His father laughed again.

"Yerushalyim? Do you know what that costs? To fly a coffin? To buy a plot? You want me to mail myself there so they can stick me in a rocky hillside in the shadow of some Western-style mall? No, not Israel, Larry. Here, in Memphis," he said. "I'm going to be buried by the *machatanim*. I'll be buried near your sister's family's plots."

"In Memphis forever?"

His father had nodded.

In Memphis, forever. Yes.

Larry didn't know what to do with this. What about the plots his parents already had back in Royal Hills?

"My wedding present to her and that fool."

"You gave your plot to Dennis?"

"The very day they exchanged rings. Let your mother rest under a shared headstone with that fool name for a Jew carved on it. 'Dennis.' It's like spending eternity buried next to a tennis coach."

"But, Dad, they're not going to come back to Brooklyn. Not ever. They don't even fly out to visit."

"What do you know about the decisions of your mother and that idiot? What podiatrist moves his business to a place where the rich sit with their feet up all day? There isn't a hard-work bunion for fifty miles from their house."

"Why are we talking about feet? You don't belong here,

Abba," Larry said, gesturing to the hospital room, and the hospital, to the city of Memphis, and the great state of Tennessee. "What if I get the plots back right now? What if I confirm with Mom? You should be buried in Royal Hills, where the Jews are. And where you've always been. You could take one and I— I could use the other."

"Yes," his father said. "Abandon us now, like it's nothing. But I'm sure you'll want to come back to us then."

At the word "abandon," Larry had winced. His father, catching it, understood. "I don't mean 'abandon' as a son, Larry. You are here. You flew down. You stay at the La Quinta Inn and do your part. A perfect child. I'm talking about as a Jew. Not me, abandoned. I mean your people, your faith. And that is also why."

"Why, what?"

"Why, here."

"Because I'm secular?"

"Because I'm dying. And when I go, I want everything done right. Done real."

IV

IT'S THE "EVERYTHING DONE RIGHT" THAT HAS RABBI RYE guiding Larry from the living room to the den. They've just finished davening on the last night of lockdown. In a clearly pre-arranged plan, Dina follows on their heels, with Duvy Huffman in tow.

Huffman is head of the *Chevreh Kaddishe*—the local burial society. This thick-necked, triple-chinned interloper was the man who'd readied their father's body for its return to dust.

Dina hadn't let anyone enter the den since their father had gone to the hospital, and then on to the grave. They were using the room for its emotional leverage, when all that remained of shivah was a single sunrise, and final minyan, after which all those gathered would call on brother and sister to arise and be comforted by God among the mourners of Zion.

Dina's husband was noticeably absent. She'd left Avi out of it, as she always did when it was time for her and Larry to roll up their sleeves and fight. Really, Avi not being there did not bode well.

Not one of the three who face Larry pretends this is spontaneous. Huffman and Rye stand on either side of Dina. Behind them, a wall of gilt- and silver-spined religious books towers over them all. Larry moves back, only to hit the frame of the open pull-out couch, the blanket still tousled, the sheets in a twist.

As for the premeditated, that jackrabbit of a rabbi, looking even more sinewy in Huffman's shadow, raises an eyebrow, giving Dina her cue.

"As you must be aware," she says, speechifying and overly formal, "tomorrow we get up, and tomorrow you fly home. And I need to know, Larry, that you understand your responsibilities as our father's only son."

"Why does everyone keep acting like I'm not Jewish?" he says, already heated. "You think I don't know the rules? You think, without you watching, I'd cremate him and stuff his ashes in a can? That I'd plant his bones in some field of crosses and pour a bottle of bourbon on the mound?"

Seeing where the conversation was too quickly headed, Rabbi Rye pipes in. "We're not talking funerals. That is already done, executed exactly according to halachah."

But Dina is ready to rumble. She takes a half step forward, blocking the rabbi's line of sight and signaling that she has things under control.

"I'm talking about what's now, Larry. I'm asking about the torch you must carry for this family—our family—for the next eleven months. Tell me you get that the Kaddish is on you."

"I get it," Larry says.

"You do? Do you really? You know you can't miss. Not once. Not a single service." She uses the English word, which Larry knows is meant to cut, to wound him for how far he's strayed. "Eight times a day, that's how many times the Kaddish gets said."

"I get that too," Larry says. "I've been here all week. Putting on tefillin. Doing my job."

"But we both know you're going to quit that job tomorrow. And I desperately need you not to, Larry." His sister's eyes are now full of pleading, and the face they plead from shocks Larry with how much older it looks, suddenly aged by their collective loss.

When the mirrors are uncovered, Larry wonders what he'll see.

"You don't have to be religious," his sister says. "You don't have to believe. You can think nothing and feel nothing and eat your cheeseburgers every meal." Here she shoots a glance to Rye, to make sure she's delivering the goods. "But you can't skip a minyan. Not once. Not ever. It's what our father expects—what he expects right now from *Olam HaBa*. Because it's that alone, what you *do*, what you *say*, that sets for our father the best conditions in the World to Come."

"It's true," Rabbi Rye says, with Huffman nodding. Then both men join Dina in what is their best approximation of her sisterly, pleading stare.

They all know Larry has no intention of spending the year in synagogue. That there's no way Larry can handle—is even interested in handling—a gargantuan commitment like that.

Larry stares back, not at his sister, but alternating between the two men. Dina has brought them to support her, and that's exactly what Larry wants them to do. Support his sister. Let them make her feel safe and secure and whole in knowing she's done her part.

As long as Larry promises he'll say the prayer, what does it hurt Dina if he skips? And, honestly, what does it hurt their dead father, in Heaven above, if Larry says a prayer or not? Does anyone really think God sits up there with a scorecard, checking off every one of Larry's blessings?

But Dina's eyes, that gaze, his sister needs to hear him say it. And so Larry does.

"I promise," he says. "I won't miss."

At that, Dina lets out a wail, heartrending. If she could have thrown herself into Rabbi Rye's arms for comfort, if these people touched outside of marriage, she'd be sobbing on his shoulder, while he stroked the wig that covers her hair.

Instead, she says to Rye, "I told you. I told you he'd say that. I tried. I did like you said."

Larry responds, as if Dina were addressing him.

"But I said Yes. That I would. I said I'd do it."

"But you're lying!" she yells, her feet solidly planted, and sort of heaving her upper body his way.

"Now, now," Rabbi Rye says to Dina, calming. "Let us not say 'lying' when we can assume goodwill. Are you lying?" he asks Larry.

"No," Larry says. "I'm not."

"You see?" the rabbi says to Dina, using a tone straight from the rabbinical playbook. "He knows, your brother, that it is a blessing such a responsibility. We all want the same for your father, that he should find a *lichtige Gan Eden,* a truly radiant afterlife. And for him to achieve this? We all know that for eleven months the Kaddish must be recited in his name."

Larry points out that they all do, in fact, know this, and had known it since childhood, and that his sister had just said it like two seconds before. He also points out that it is really insulting to even pretend to need to restate it for everyone's benefit.

And it is for just this moment that Duvy Huffman was recruited. Because anyone who'd made a condolence call had seen how short and crabby and plain angry Larry seemed with his sister. And every Jew in town, including Rye himself, knew that, as effective a clergyman as he was, when the good rabbi wasn't preaching to the like-minded, hook-line-and-sinker crowd, he was without any charm at all. And so, to Duvy, it falls.

"What the rabbi and your sister are trying to say," Duvy says, "what they mean—"

"Yes," the rabbi says. "Tell him what we mean."

Under pressure, Huffman tilts his head this way and that, while his thoughts line up. "The concern is that you might tell us you'll do something, while really feeling it is none of our business what you actually do. You may be thinking, 'What does it matter? Who, in the end, will be the wiser?'"

What a fine interpreter the rabbi and Dina have chosen! What a good translator of intent they've found in Duvy Huffman. For that is just exactly what Larry is thinking to himself.

"It is this worry," Duvy says, raising his voice an octave, "that has your sister using harsh words and has the rabbi, inadvertently, condescending. It's not for me that I inquire again, but for your father. We're just trying to surmise, to get at the veracity—"

"Of my commitment? Which I've just made?"

Huffman thinks about it, while Dina stands with her arms crossed, seething.

"If you are only promising so as to get us off your back," Duvy says, "then we ask, please, at the very least, tell it like it is. Shoot straight. So that we may find an honest starting point for what is a very important conversation."

Now it is Larry's turn to consider. He takes his time doing it, and Rye, he can't handle the silence.

"The Kaddish. Every time you utter it," Rye says, "it affects your father's status in the World to Come. It literally affects his *neshamah* in the place where he may, this very second, be gathering wood for his own fire."

That, it does Larry in.

"Are you nuts? You think my dad is gathering sticks to burn himself?"

"It's maybe a metaphor, the wood," Rabbi Rye says, raising his hands in the air.

"And the fire?" Larry wants to know.

"Fire is fire." Rye wears an expression that says, "I cannot lie."

"You're really crazy. All of you. And the sins of the son don't go up to the father! That's not how it works."

"In some instances they do. For the child under bar mitzvah age, say, that would be an example of an upward pass." Rabbi Rye steps behind Dina as Larry tenses, red with rage. "But that's not what we're discussing," he says over Dina's shoulder. "In this case. Here it's not negative. It's beautiful. It raises you up. And raises your father up. It even raises up God! As Rashi tells us—"

"No Rashi!" Larry yells back. "No opinions. No commentaries. No stories. Just facts! Our dad, he was the purest, kindest, most selfless man," Larry says, looking now at a responsive Dina, drawing her in. "Do you really think, if I sleep in one morning—"

And he watches as his sister's face falls.

"You'll sleep in every morning!" she yells. "You're not going to daven. Just admit it."

"It can't matter. It can't," Larry says, trying to organize his argument, to lift it above the roiling emotions, to give voice to his beliefs. "If there's God, for real, it can't possibly matter to our father's afterlife what I do here. That's not—it can't be— how it works."

From his sister comes a piteous "It is. It is. It is." She reaches out, she takes her brother's wrists, lightly, with love. "It was his wish," she says. "He loved you so much. But our father was terrified that you'd let him down."

"No," Larry says, shaking his head.

"That's the last thing he said to me in this life. 'The Kaddish. Don't let your brother let me down.'"

In front of these two men. The sheer size of it.

To his sister, Larry says, "He didn't. I was there." And then, for good measure, he adds a "Fuck you."

The men recoil. But Dina, she has been his big sister for a very long time.

"Big shot," she says, dropping his wrists.

"You are merciless, Dina. Really, go fuck yourself. Or let horny Avi help you, you monster."

Huffman, drained of color, steadies himself against the rabbi, a hand on his shoulder for support.

Still, a brave man, Duvy speaks. "To be dying and afraid no one will say the prayer over you, it is a serious matter."

Larry takes Huffman's measure. He looks even shorter and fatter standing next to that gristly Rye. He deserves, Larry feels, a "Fuck you too!" but Larry does not deliver it.

What he says instead is, "It mattered deeply to my father. But he didn't die afraid. Not because of me. As cruel as it is to insinuate—"

"I didn't insinuate," his sister says. "I stated it. Because I know."

"I was with him too," Larry says, "and he went happy. He went in peace, knowing who I really am." Larry practically cries. "I'm a good boy! He told me himself."

They stare at him, with nothing less than compassion. Sad specimen that he is.

Dina asks him again, this time calmly, "Will you promise to do it, to say your prayers?"

"I won't promise and I won't pray," Larry says. "Not with a group, and not by myself. I'll do it at home when I'm in the mood. I'll honor my father *my* way. And I believe—just like you believe things—that it's just as good."

"But it isn't," his sister says, despairing. "And God made you the one—the only one for the job."

"But why?" Larry says. "Why can't you do it, Dina? Why don't you say the fucking prayers? If you're the person in this family Dad could trust, if he gave you his fucking body to keep, then take on the responsibility that comes with. Say the Kaddish yourself."

"I'm a girl!" she says. "I can't."

"For one, you're a woman," Larry says. "For two, fix your religion." To Rabbi Rye, he says, "It's nonsense to stay in the fucking Dark Ages. Make it even. It's 1999. It's time. Fix your community. Let her say the Kaddish!" The rabbi looks openly pained and drops down onto the edge of the open couch bed. "Come on, Rabbi," Larry says. "Tell her it's OK, so that it will be OK. Be the first brave rabbi to allow it."

"This is not how it works," Rye says.

Larry turns to Huffman. "What about you, Duvy? Why don't you try to make smart the rabbi's backwards position? Tart it up for us. Make it look good."

"It isn't backwards," Duvy says.

"Great." Larry addresses his sister, as if the others are no longer there. "Why not have Avi do it? 'A second son,' is what Dad always called him. He already prays like fifty times a day."

"Avi's my husband. He's not blood!"

"So your boy, then."

"You want to hear cursing, hotshot?" his sister says. "You want to hear a foul mouth, you sick fuck of a brother? You want a child to mourn instead of you? He's not even in line. No, Larry. You're the one."

"Well, then I guess our father's going to Hell."

And with that, Larry finds the emotional pressure point he didn't know he'd been after. Dina begins wailing, unhinged.

When she gains control of her sobbing, she says, "When you want to be mean, little brother, there's no one more brutal."

"Really? Because that's nothing compared to telling me our father died afraid—because of me."

"Then prove him wrong," Dina says, "and do your part!"

"I will. I swear it," he says. "But I'll do it my way."

His sister looks right then to the rabbi, who has somehow floated back to his feet. His sister turns to this man, and the institution he represents, hoping for salvation.

Larry joins her, the two of them finally on the same side. "Yes. Fix it, Rabbi." he says. "Let's see what you've got."

Rabbi Rye breathes so deeply that his chest puffs out, pigeon-like. He seems suddenly different, ready for the challenge. With a considered pull to his beard, he seems to Larry truly rabbinical for the first time.

"On your father's side?" Rye asks. "There are no siblings left?"

"No one," Larry's sister says. "No men in any direction, just this one useless son. The only man. Only he's not man enough."

The rabbi gives another few strokes to his beard, as if to tame it.

"You could," the rabbi says, "you could *yotzei* someone else, in an emergency like this. You could assign a kind of *shaliach mitzvah*—like an emissary. A proxy to say it in your staid."

"A proxy?" Dina says. "Even with this one right here, alive?"

"The Kaddish getting said is all that matters. First we try the best case. Then we problem-solve from there."

"So her husband could," Larry says, "if he wanted—"

"Not Avi," Dina says. "Not my husband. You want a proxy, you find a proxy." To Rabbi Rye, she says, "But if he finds some-one else, that would really be kosher? Fully? Same as if he said it himself?"

"Fully and totally. A thousand percent kosher if the per-son who's saying it doesn't miss and keeps your father in his prayers. Don't spread it around, but it really is—halachically— the same."

Sister looks to brother. Brother looks to sister.

And Dina nods her ascent.

"You figure it out, Larry. Tonight. Or I will chain you to the bed. You understand? If I don't know it's being said you're not getting out of my sight."

Dina turns to Rabbi Rye. "If it's as kosher as you say, Rabbi, then I can live with it. But the obligation to see it through, it stays on him. Let my brother take responsibility for once in his *gornisht* life. For once, let him fix his own fucking mess."

V

HERE LIES LARRY WITH HIS BURDEN UPON HIM. HOW would he find someone to say the Kaddish in his stead?

He knows he's irrational from exhaustion, from despair and grief, from being in his sister's space and stripped of his routines. If only he could sleep for a little. If only he could make it to morning, he'd tackle the problem head-on.

Also, if he sleeps soon, he might not lose his mind.

But to sleep, Larry knows, he needs a release. For nearly a week, despite his small rebellions, he's smoked neither cigarette nor joint, he hasn't had a stiff drink (or three), he hasn't once sunk into the living-room couch to binge eat and binge watch, gorging on junk (visual and edible) until the stomach acid burned and his brain conked out.

Larry had even abstained from his digital diversions—no e-mails, no games, and, beyond his useless nephew-aimed maritime search, he'd refrained from surfing the Web. He'd done nothing that offered him pleasure or escape. And wasn't that what shivah was about, after all?

Thinking himself down this path is, he knows, a classic example of Larry-like cowardice and dissociation, the epitome of his unwillingness to engage with his own most intimate thoughts.

If he was pondering relief, and searching for escape, and honestly just hankering for some rest, the list in Larry's head would be one entry long. What he most definitely hadn't done since his father's passing was the thing he couldn't admit he was about to do now.

It had taken Larry years of post-religious, practiced focus to turn off the Godly eyes, and the dear-and-departed eyes, so that, steeped in his depravity, he might feel himself unseen. But since his father's loss, he hasn't once pornified, unable to shake the ghostly feeling of his newly dead father looking down.

If he didn't feel his own life hanging in the balance, if he didn't believe that, without releasing the pressure, he, himself, might drop dead in his nephew's narrow bed, Larry would not, under Dina's roof, succumb.

Larry fires up his laptop and clicks on his browser. Headphoneless, he mutes the volume and types in a site. Then, with deep breath and dramatic pause, Larry hits enter, flooding his sister's pious home with the world's filthiest filth.

WHEN LARRY COMES, HE SUFFERS SUCH GUILT AND SUCH shame that he can't even bear the way those fish flit around, gawking at him, full of judgment. Hoping to distract those terrible creatures, Larry goes over to the tank. He opens the top and grabs the fish food, those sodden tissues still balled up in his hand.

He shakes the smelly tin and, amid a snow of flakes, a sizable dollop of sperm drops into the tank.

Larry watches as that blob hits the surface, immediately transforming into a kind of viscous, tendriled sea creature and beginning its watery descent.

Setting down tin and tissues, Larry races for the net. But it's too late. Those fish, they are all already upon it, pecking away with their puckered fish mouths and fish lips. It—that bit of Larry—is gobbled up, and gone, in an instant.

Larry wants to cry as he rids himself of the remaining evidence and creeps back into bed. In his misery, he's surprised to discover that, more than the crushing embarrassment, it's the warm and fuzzy chemicals released that are winning the battle inside his brain.

Suddenly relaxed, suddenly sleepy, suddenly (despite it all) unburdened, Larry opens a new browser window (clicking off the porn-soused one whose tiny tabs peek up behind). Feeling inspired, he begins googling his way toward a solution for all that ails. Pausing in this fugue state to be horrified by the source of his newfound vision, Larry manages what is for him a rare and very different kind of self-love. He forgives.

Is it anyway anyone's business from whence comes a person's inspiration? What matters is that he finds what he's looking for. The answer to his prayers.

Who ever thought the solution to his, and his sister's, and the spirit of their father's intractable problem might be reached by melding all their disparate beliefs?

For the Internet and new technology is the answer, and tradition is the answer, and that spread-to-the-corners-of-the-earth idea of a linked and universal Jewish home ends up being the answer too.

Larry had chanced upon a website based in Jerusalem, and

behind that website was a yeshiva, and behind that place of study was a group of deeply committed students who—a paid service—would say the Mourner's Prayer.

Sharing the worry that plagued Rabbi Rye and Duvy Huffman, that tore at the heart of Larry's dear sister, and that rested on Larry's fat head, these young scholars were offering a resource designed to spare the innocent, forsaken soul from the heat of a cleansing hellfire.

Larry laughs out loud. All that time searching only to land on an address that Larry, on instinct alone, should have entered at the start: kaddish.com.

To sign up, one filled out a form with the name of the deceased, his or her birthday and death day, their likes and dislikes. Then there was a space for biographical information, and any anecdotes or representative memories that might better muster a portrait of the departed.

According to the FAQ page, upon receiving the application, the site's administrator would create a profile to circulate among the available students, finding the perfect match for the fallen. It was like a JDate for the dead.

He'd have thought it harder to choose the stories that best described his father, to rattle off preferences, summoning for strangers the true heart of the man. In engaging with a flood of memories, Larry feels closer to his father, and more at peace with his passing, than he has since his death.

Larry submits the application and then waits exactly ten seconds before checking his e-mail for a reply. When none appears, Larry refreshes in an endless cycle, tapping at the trackpad to his heart's content. When he's had his Skinner-box fill, Larry finally clicks the window closed, satisfied on a number of fronts.

WOE IS TO LARRY, FOR HIS SHORT-LIVED COMFORT. THE kaddish.com page snaps closed only to reveal a window lurking behind. It had been there the whole time, waiting, while Larry so lovingly filled out the form.

Larry's pop-up blocker had failed him. And so he's thrust from the purity of his reminiscence into the crude, crude reality of his life. A woman stares back at Larry through the ether. She's busy with—and what can Larry do but call it what it is?—a lubriciously large glass dildo.

The tool itself is so outsized that when inserted and thoroughly swallowed up, Larry feels like he's looking into the woman's very core. It's as if, pondering death, he's now gazing straight back to life's start, to the place that Larry's college art history professor—with the lights of the lecture hall off, and a provocation of a Courbet painting projected on a screen—had introduced as *The Origin of the World.*

Larry's eyes again shift to the woman's to see what she might be thinking herself. All he gets is simulated eye contact and simulated orgasm, as she moans in muted silence, trapped in her digitized, teaser loop. A perpetual, shared moment that was for this woman surely one thing, and for Larry another. Except right then, it isn't for Larry what it usually would be. He isn't titillated, only numb, forcing him to reconcile how desensitized he's become.

He'd stared at similar scenes with such frequency and regularity that this one just seems prolapsedly, membranously, fistedly mundane. No different than switching on a baseball game after getting home from a doubleheader. It allows Larry to register that this performer, trapped in time, had, at some point, pulled on her clothes and gone home, worn out and exhausted from doing what was nothing more than her terrible job.

Would his sister pass out if she walked in on Larry and saw such a feed? Would she scratch out her saintly eyes, trying to unsee? Larry is sure that as modern as Dina fancies herself, she doesn't have the slightest idea of the everyday depravities filling the alternate reality that ate more and more of sad Larry's time.

And then it strikes him, a giant truth for Larry to absorb.

While dutifully enacting the pledge he'd taken before his sister and her two kosher witnesses, while recording remembrances of his father so that a devout yeshiva student might better know the man behind the page, in and out, in and out, that glass dildo dipped.

That downtrodden woman, a fake smile on her face, had worked her apparatus, as if she'd been turned, for whatever paltry payment, into a human butter churn, God help her. And God help me, Larry thinks. Then—for the first time since he'd left the fold—a personal, heartfelt prayer escapes his lips.

"God protect my father's soul."

LARRY EATS HIS CHEERIOS IN THE MORNING WHILE WATCHing the men assemble for prayers. He finishes his breakfast, and then, with a borrowed tallis, and borrowed tefillin, holding a siddur whose pages were worn smooth by another person's hands, he follows along.

With one sincere, Larry-generated prayer already loosed, he goes for another. He prays that they might find him a match in Jerusalem—whatever the price.

After davening, as he's about to be released from shivah to stroll around the block, Larry excuses himself and hurries straight to his nephew's room. He takes his filthy, corrupted laptop and checks his mail again.

And there it is, a letter from the site. It initially appears to be an apology, which nearly stops Larry's heart. What could anyone be sorry for, but not being able to rescue him from his plight? But, no, the site's administrator is only sorry that the choices are not greater, though he wants Larry to know, the one student available is a truly special young man, eager to do the job.

Attached is a picture of the boy with his hand to his forehead, as he stares down at a holy book. Larry can see a wispy black beard, and the side curls tucked behind his ears. There's just enough of his mouth visible in shadow for Larry to believe he sees a warm smile.

Larry reads the letter from the student that comes after the administrator's introduction. It is beautiful, if only two lines. "Dear Sir, I understand the responsibility that comes with the task I'm about to undertake. Know that, as you are his son, so, for the next eleven months, am I. Sincerely, Chemi."

There's a link to click that takes Larry to a rudimentarily animated page displaying a contract, and a pen. Off to the side is a disembodied hand, clasping and unclasping.

Larry is prompted to sign, and does so. A flashing arrow then has him drag the pen to the hand, which closes around it.

All Larry's religious learning comes bubbling to the surface. He understands immediately that the hand is meant to be Chemi's and the pen his, that this transfer is a digital form of *kinyan*. It's a symbolic exchange, to which the Kaddish is attached.

Larry cries and cries, racking sobs that do not abate for some time. He suddenly feels the true weight of the duty that was, and always had been, his—though he'd just now passed it off to another.

Having found a way to meet his obligation "halachically," as the rabbi said, having found a way to do it "right" and "real," as his father had wanted, Larry wipes his nose and takes out his credit card, entering the numbers. Sealing the deal with Chemi, Larry clicks "purchase" and pays.

part two

VI

WAS IT A WEEK AFTER THE CONTRACT ENDED, WAS IT two, that Larry had received an envelope postmarked from Jerusalem and sent to his apartment in Clinton Hill? He'd torn it open to find a letter, along with a black-and-white photo of a student, who he immediately recognized, though the young man was shot from behind.

Snapping open the page, the letter was comprised of a single typed line. Oh, that efficient Chemi! It said, only, "It's been an honor to be your emissary, mourning the dead in your name."

Where a piece of correspondence would usually be signed "Sincerely," or "All Best," the boy had written *"Chayim Aruchim"*—Long Life—spelled out in English characters.

It was not the clipped and economical note but the photograph that had started Larry crying in a way he hadn't since enrolling with kaddish.com.

In the picture, Chemi sat alone in a modest study hall poring over a *blat* of Gemara. There were a couple of long tables, an arched window, and a section of a peeling, domed ceiling that looked no broader than a teacup. And though no fixture was visible hanging from above, a circle of light illuminated the student and his book.

He remembers admiring how deeply Chemi was embroiled in his learning and—this is the point that matters—he remembers thinking it exactly as he recalls it now: "Look at that boy's focus!" is what he'd thought. "See how this young man, alone in the *beit midrash*, struggles to *assimilate* some Talmudic idea."

Back then, Larry had cried for how moving he found the image of study to be, which then had him crying for his father, a year gone from this world.

As Larry's crying turned to weeping, he'd understood that he was no longer weeping for any of those things. The tears shed were not over a lost father. The tears he'd spilled were for his lost self.

That, at least, is what he came to believe in the ensuing weeks, and months, the ensuing years, and—could it be?—the two decades that followed. It is the version of events he held on to after he'd again taken on his Hebrew name, going back to Shaul, before settling on the nickname Shuli (a nod to Chemi, he felt). It was the "lost soul" narrative that Larry had first told himself, before repeating his story of rebirth to countless others.

"Do you know what is the subconscious?" Shuli might ask his seventh-grade students. "Do you understand the complicated inner workings of the mind?"

He raises these same questions when he's brought in to inspire at a *kumzitz*, or a *Shabbaton*, or any kind of gathering of the faithful and, even more so, when addressing those who might want to be.

He performs the story almost weekly at his Friday night table, at the *Shabbos* dinners, where there is always a guest or two invited for *kiruv*. Those secular Jews with a budding interest in their own lost traditions, willing to open themselves up to outreach, and the kind of inspired personal myth with which a born-again man like Reb Shuli might regale them.

"Don't you think it's funny," he says, "that I saw the photo of this student, this Chemi, leaning over a table working on some Talmudic problem, and did not just think, 'Oh, look, at that young man studying'? I didn't just think, 'The boy sits there, and *he* thinks.' What could be a simpler way to put it?" Shuli doesn't wait for an answer.

"It wasn't 'wondering,' or 'sussing out.' It wasn't 'embroiled in' or 'reflecting upon' or 'pondering' that came to my addled mind. Of all the possibilities in our rich language, what I thought was, 'There he sits, *assimilating.*'" Shuli stands and raises a finger up with such emphasis that the *Shabbos* candles flicker in its wake.

"Could there be a more perfect choice of words?" Shuli asks. He steps back from the table, as if stepping away from the power of his own story.

"There I was, alone on my couch, in *goyishe* Clinton Hill, thinking, 'Over there in Jerusalem sits Chemi assimilating the Talmud—assimilating information precisely as *Hashem, HaKadosh Baruch Hu,* intends—and me, what am I doing in my empty life here? What kind of assimilation is mine?'"

WITH THAT PHOTO BEFORE HIM, SHULI HAD OPENED HIMself up to certain possibilities, ignoring how embarrassing exploring those possibilities would, in practice, be.

Back at the beginning of his transformation, his sister ended up playing a pivotal role. Without forcing him to acknowledge anything openly, she provided Larry with the cover he desperately craved.

When visiting his sister's house in Memphis—far from the prying eyes of his irreligious, heterogeneous Brooklyn gang—Larry could quite naturally play by Dina's rules.

During that period of tentative re-exploration, Larry would simply fly down for the weekend and, embodying his usual role of secular, black-sheep uncle, and under the guise of being a good sport, put on a yarmulke when joining the family for meals. And once the yarmulke was on, it was no great leap to leave it on, to maybe borrow a suit jacket from Avi on *Shabbos* morning, so that he could, while holding hands with a niece or nephew, accompany the family on their walk to shul.

From there, all unfolded speedily, and with utter ease. And why shouldn't it have, when he'd rediscovered his one, true self?

Shuli asks this rhetorically of his dinner guests, as he opens another bottle of wine with a dramatic, cork-pulling, punctuating pop.

In the end, Larry's transmogrification back into Shuli couldn't have been any more ordinary. As his dear, wise father had said; as his too-smart-for-her-own-good, meddling sister had pointed out; as he himself had finally understood: His return and redemption were the most conventional things that could happen to the stray child in any family. What else was Shuli doing but coming home?

And it was not only home to his sister, and not only home to his faith, but Shuli was returning home-home, to Royal Hills, Brooklyn. He soon traced his way back the three subway stops, toward the stand-alone aluminum-sided houses, toward the worser restaurants, and his fellow Jews.

Shuli returned to the heart of the community he'd grown up in. He sold his Clinton Hill apartment for about a thousand times what he paid for it, so that he was able to afford a modest house in the neighborhood in which he'd grown up. He'd used the windfall to pay for his own years of study, until he was living on the salary of a seventh-grade Gemara teacher at the very yeshiva where he had gone. When there was a wife, which— after meeting Miri, his *bashert*—there very soon was, he was able to support her as well when she'd stopped her own high-school teaching to learn all day. It had been important to them both that one of them be able to dedicate their life, full-time, to Torah study. And, as Shuli put it, it was no coin flip to see—between the two—who had a better mind. So Miri learned at the women's *kollel*.

This is the arrangement they continued to balance when the happy couple was blessed first with a girl and then with a boy, two children, born two years in a row.

With his teaching job and that Clinton Hill Buffer (which is what he and Miri called that ever-dwindling resource) Shuli was able to keep them all fed and clothed, and put the whole family in shiny new shoes every year at the holidays. A gift from God, that extra money. A sign that he'd done what's right.

And on a night like this, when his guests do not ask for the takeaway at the end of Reb Shuli's inspiring story, he offers it himself, with a blushing pride and bearded smile.

Having refilled all the glasses, Reb Shuli remains on his feet. He nods toward his wife, and then goes over to the side of the table where his children sit across from the guests. He hugs Hayim, his son, age eight, and Nava, his daughter of nine. He then stands behind them, a palm pressed atop each of their heads, fingers waggling, as they laugh—so much different than when he'd laid hands upon them for their weekly blessing, earlier in the night. He looks to his Miri, lovingly, and she, lovingly, looks back. And he says to those welcome guests, "I do not share the story to brag, or show off, or even to make excuses for all the years of lost time. I only share it to say, it's never too late to live one's true life."

VII

ONE'S TRUE LIFE! COULD SHULI POSSIBLY LOVE HIS ANY more? He feels grateful always. Even when marching toward his classroom to deal with a troubled student who—a fifty-fifty chance—awaits. Reb Shuli carries with him the relevant *masechta* of Gemara in one hand and a barrel-sized mug of coffee in the other. Sipping at it in the hallway, he steels himself with a sigh.

He attends to this headache of a boy during recess. Shuli would bet it never crosses the boys' minds that when he takes their playtime away, it's also his own recess that he's losing.

Peering through the wire-mesh window in the door, Reb Shuli is thrilled to see Gavriel already seated, with his small student chair pulled right up to the other side of Shuli's desk. He wouldn't have believed it possible, to see a student such as this, not only waiting, but waiting patiently—Gavriel straight-backed and unfidgety.

He looks the perfect angel.

In light of this, Shuli alters his body language as he steps into the room. He does not look so stern as he might have, relaxing his shoulders and putting to rest his furry, overgrown eyebrows, which he'd already set in motion, hoping for a sort of punitive, caterpillar-like wave.

He struggles then to find a replacement expression. How many directions can the mouth tilt, or the forehead wrinkle, to tip off a feeling? In his case, not many. Which reminds Shuli of his dear sister and her signature judgmental look. God had, in these middle-age years, given Shuli his bushy eyebrows. And to Dina, at birth, those rolling eyes.

"So, *nu?*" Shuli says, opening with the default rabbinical gambit.

He places his mug and Talmud in the middle of the desk. He sits and pops the hat from his head, resting it a safe distance from the coffee, crown down.

Gavriel doesn't blink, acknowledging nothing. Not his general jokiness and disruptions, nor the faces Reb Shuli can feel burning the back of his neck whenever he turns to write on the board. He doesn't say a thing about the grave wrong with which he had to know he was about to be charged.

Matching silence with silence seems the best route. Shuli leans back in his chair while the sounds of the missed recess pour in from the playground.

The boy looks wronged as he waits his rebbe out.

Shuli wants to tell Gavriel that he doesn't know how good he has it. Yeshiva boys today, what consequences do they face? Rob a bank during school hours, and still, you'll end up across from a teacher like Shuli, talking about the roots of your feelings.

It's his father's story that Shuli wants to share.

On *Shabbos* afternoons, when Shuli was little, he would sit on his father's lap while his father read. Restless, he'd play with his father's tie and then his father's face, trying to distract him. Always he'd get to his ears, the left one of which a tiny Reb Shuli would run his fingers across, delighted.

For this ear was not perfectly smooth, as ears tend to be. There was a sort of jagged indentation, a divot in the curve at the top.

He'd ask his father about it, though he'd heard the story a hundred times. His father would laugh and tell him again. For his father found it as silly in the reciting as Shuli did in the hearing.

His father would tell him that, back in school, he'd sometimes been a naughty boy himself—even fathers could be. One day, he'd interrupted the class, upsetting his rebbe with some infraction he couldn't recall, no matter how often Shuli begged his father to try.

The teacher had explained to his father that, when you steal even one minute of Torah, it is not just your minute lost. It is multiplied by each person present—one minute taken from every student in the room. According to this calculation, Reb Shuli's father had actually stolen eighteen minutes of Torah learning that would never reach God's ears.

And while his father processed this concept, his rebbe had taken up his ruler and, in front of the class, struck his father a blow to the ear so hard that it broke—putting a dent in the cartilage that never went away. Always at that point in the telling, as little Shuli felt that ear with his fingers, his father would feel the spot himself.

"Do you know what happened?" his father would ask him. "Do you know what happened when I got home?"

"What?" Shuli would say.

"I ran to my mother, to tell her how the rabbi had beat me. I ran to show her my broken ear. And do you know what my mother did?"

"What?" Shuli would ask, already giggling.

"She said, 'If he hit you a *zetz* like that, you must have done something terrible.' Then she beat me, a second time, for my sins."

This they both found fully entertaining, horribly unjust as it was.

Shuli laughs at the memory, and this is what gets the boy talking. Gavriel asks him why.

Reb Shuli shifts his weight forward so that the chair creaks. "What? You sit there quiet, and I'm supposed to tell you my secrets?"

And like that Shuli watches him clam up.

"I laughed because I was being nostalgic," Shuli says. "It's what happens when you're old. But we're not here to figure me out. This is so we can understand what's going on with you, and why you do the things you do."

"Which things?"

"You tell me."

And again, there's silence.

"Listen, I'm not here to punish, or make trouble. I'm here because I see a miserable kid, getting more miserable and acting out. And what I want is to see you happy and maybe, *chas v'chalilah*, even having a good time"

"That's why you're here? To see me happy?"

"Fair enough," Reb Shuli says. "I'm here to see you happy and also to address some things. There's a rumor that has come to me. Others—your peers—they say that maybe you didn't study for Friday's test. That maybe, God forbid, you tore the page from the Gemara itself and taped it inside your desk—not only cheating, but desecrating something holy, as would the enemies of Israel."

"They said that?"

"They did," Reb Shuli admits, as much as it pains him. "But I told those who whispered, I said, 'I know this Gavriel. He is a good person, with a kind heart.' I told them, 'It's impossible that he'd do such a terrible thing, and it must be you boys making up nonsense.'" Reb Shuli, satisfied with his delivery, gives a good tickle to his own chin, hidden beneath his beard. "You know, I could ask for your copy of the *masechta* myself, to check for the missing page. But why would I want to try to prove something that I already know can't be true?"

The boy turns red, squirming in his seat.

"Can I go now?"

"Soon. After we spend a little while studying a *daf* that you maybe didn't learn so well."

The boy turns his eyes toward the ceiling, as if he can see the sounds of recess gathering above and raining down.

Shuli joins him in looking up, while pulling his chair around to Gavriel's side of the desk. He then opens his Gemara and presses his finger to the *Tosafot*.

With that finger steady, Reb Shuli finally draws the boy's gaze to his own, only to find tears swimming in Gavriel's eyes.

"Would you like to tell me what else is going on? You can't be this sad because you're missing out on kicking a ball."

"On the weekend," Gavriel says, "when my mother was gone, I took money from her drawer—I stole it. And then I went to the corner, to the store, and I ate *treif*."

"*Treif!*" Reb Shuli says, truly startled, the confession catching him off guard.

"A candy I wanted to taste. I ate it."

"Why even do such a thing when there are so many kosher candies? Why not eat one you're allowed?"

"Theirs," the boy says, meaning the Gentiles', "theirs look so much better than ours."

"So you wanted to know?"

The boy nods, and a tear falls onto Shuli's desk.

"So, *nu?*" Reb Shuli says. "How do they taste?"

"So much better," the boy says, his voice full of despair.

Reb Shuli laughs a heartfelt bellow of a laugh.

It's inappropriate for him to tell the child that, yes, their food tastes so much better. That Shuli had, for many years, lived—and eaten—in their world.

What he says instead is "Sometimes things are as we expect them to be. You had to know, and now you do."

Reb Shuli closes the book and leans in close to the child. "Rabbis, we are not priests. We don't have to hear your secrets to fix you. We don't dispense forgiveness on God's behalf."

The boy stares blankly and maybe also curiously. The tears are gone from his eyes.

"You steal," Shuli says. "You eat a candy that you shouldn't. You maybe even—I don't believe it—cheat and tear a page. So what? Who cares? It's not the troublemaking that matters. It's the sadness behind it. That's what I want to fix. Is it the *yetzer hara* doing this? What's in you?" Shuli asks, terrified the recess bell will ring at this critical juncture. Time is not on his side. "I'm asking seriously. Do you feel driven by the evil inclination? Or is it just ants in your pants?"

"In my pants?" the boy says, confused.

"I'm saying, I've seen you be better and be happier. I've seen you look at a challenge in the Gemara, and then your hand shoots up with the answer. I want to know what happened to that kid." When Gavriel offers nothing, Shuli talks *tachlis*. "You think I don't know what it means when the others rat you out? Are you getting bullied? Do you have any friends? Is that the issue?"

"Not so many. But it's not that."

"All year, it's been like this with you. I've asked your other teachers, and they see it too. Did something happen over the summer, maybe at camp?"

"I guess," the boy says, "when the boys were away, and, you know, in the same bunk—"

"You weren't in the bunk?"

"I was."

"So why say 'when the boys were away'?"

"I was with them the first month—in the bunk. When my father died, my mother came up to get me."

Reb Shuli feels his head shaking back and forth of its own volition, a physical rejection to what he'd just heard, manifesting as a sort of odd tremor.

Reb Shuli tries to stop his head rattling atop the stalk of his neck—literally pressing his hands to his temples. He fights to act his normal self, while feeling as blindsided in a classroom as he'd ever been.

The child's father dead. Such a thing for Reb Shuli not to know.

It was a failure of the system. How did the mother not call— God help her? Or if she did, even worse, how might the *rosh yeshiva* not have filled the boy's *rabanim* in on the tragic news?

And what of his friends, who don't share that, but have time to tattle about cheating?

As he settles himself, Shuli blames no one, and nothing, beyond the curse of living in a big city.

If the yeshiva was in some small town, they'd all be buried at the same graveyard. They'd all pray at the same shul. The loss of a father would be shared by everyone. But here, in Royal Hills, his poor, hyperactive Gavriel swipes his student MetroCard to make his way on public transportation to Royal Hills every day. This child, commuting from Midwood. It might as well be the moon.

Even so, how could it be that Gavriel does not stand up at school when it is time to acknowledge the dead during morning and afternoon worship? He sits through the Kaddish, like all the fortunate living-fathered boys.

Reb Shuli says, *"Baruch dayan emet,"* an invocation for the deceased. Then he says, *"Tanchumai,"* offering his condolences. "I did not know," he says. "I'm so sorry. You have brothers and sisters, yes?"

"You taught two of them."

"Way back," Shuli says. "Yisroel and Leib. They are much older than you."

"I'm the youngest by six years."

"Was it a surprise, the death?" Reb Shuli instantly regrets how the question came out and asks Gavriel more gently, "Did you have any idea, before camp, that your father was ill?"

"He was having heart attacks."

"More than one?"

"He was supposed to be OK for the summer. Then he had a pulmonary embolism."

The boy sounds as grown-up as the rabbi has ever heard him. For this child even to know such a term, a *shanda*.

Shuli looks to the clock on the back wall. It was a charm in the necklace of pictures that circled the room. All the great rabbis, framed and hung to inspire this new generation.

He watches the second hand move its last short stretch. Then the bell rings, calling the others inside and signaling an end to this, the first round of their match.

"Can we talk again?" Reb Shuli asks. "There are some important things I want to discuss."

"Like what?"

Here a laugh seems to Shuli appropriate, and so he laughs. The directness with which this child operates, it was a joy.

"Fair enough," Shuli says, yet again. "I want to explain how, though you and your friends are all young and I am old . . . or you are all gangly and fast, and I am turning fat and hairy-eared and slow . . . I want you to know that you may think I'm the one most different from you in this room, but there is one thing that makes us the same."

"That we have no fathers?"

"That we have no fathers. Yes."

"That's it?"

"No. That's not all of it."

"It kind of sounds like it will be."

"And yet, it isn't," Reb Shuli says.

Gavriel stands up and begins to scrape his chair along the floor toward his desk. Reb Shuli—surprising himself—grabs the boy's arm.

"Sorry," Reb Shuli says, letting the arm go. "I just. I was thinking—how about this? What if I give a double recess tomorrow. . . ." Then, shaking his head (this time of his own volition), Shuli raises a hand and wipes the first offer away. "No, no. What if it's a triple? If I give an extra recess to make up for the one you missed today, and then the regular one for tomorrow, and then a third, so that I won't steal a minute of your playtime while we meet. Does that sound fair?"

"I guess," the boy says, making perfect sense of it. "Fine."

And like that, the others tumble through the door.

VIII

S HULI STRUGGLES THROUGH HIS DAY OF TEACHING, DIS-
tracted. He says nothing in front of his own children that evening. He acts his normal fatherly self at bedtime, though he asks
for an extra kiss and hug. And what father wouldn't, haunted by
the notion of his early demise?

In bed, he lies with a book on his chest, waiting for Miri. She
comes out of the bathroom in a long nightgown. To Shuli, it
looks as if she's floating as she moves his way.

He opens his mouth and then thinks better of it. What news
does he actually have to offer? An update on a student? A half
story? Some conversation he'd only just started when the bell
brought it to an end?

If he dragged every schoolboy sadness and disappointment
into their bedroom, if he carried home every trouble, like a cat
with a bird in its mouth, what kind of gift would that be to drop
at Miri's feet every night? When would they ever find peace?

He tells himself that nothing bad has happened. That there's
nothing worth sharing as he and Miri lay side by side.

He stares up at the ceiling, trying to feel heartened about the next morning, excited to talk to Gavriel about the choices the boy has lately made. Shuli lies like that, forcibly trying to cheer himself, until Miri begs him to turn off the light.

"I'm thinking," he tells her.

"And I'm tired," she says. "Think in the dark."

"I'm looking at the ceiling—it calms me."

"Then look at it in the dark. It'll be the same. There's nothing, on a ceiling, to see."

Reb Shuli takes his pillow down to the living room to look at a different patch of ceiling, and to pull from the shelves any books that might have the wisdom he's seeking.

After some hours, Shuli hears the creak of the floorboards, and then sees Miri's bare feet on the stairs. She stops midway, leaning over the banister and addressing him from above.

"You need to sleep, Shuli," she says. "You have the Weider wedding tomorrow, after school. A tired rabbi doesn't make a nice ceremony."

The very mention of the obligation makes Shuli want to scream.

"I told them I'm only staying through the chuppah. As soon as the *chassan* stomps on the glass, we're gone."

"Well, I ran into Daphna Weider, and she asked if we'd stay and eat, and bring the kids. I think it'll do you good. There are extra tables. And you can't say no to the mother of the bride."

This turns Shuli despondent, and Miri goes over to sit beside him on the couch.

"What is it, husband?" she says.

Like that, Shuli tells her everything that has transpired. He takes his wife's hand and gazes at her, calmed just watching her process what he's shared.

He can see that she's doing what she does best when a problem overwhelms him—Miri organizing his addled thoughts, lining them up in her head, so that she might help her poor husband think straight.

Miri says, "You're upset that you didn't know the boy's father was dead?"

Shuli nods.

"And you're also upset to learn that this child is now fatherless, his mother a widow?"

Shuli nods.

"And you are, of course, unsettled to learn that your student—a death from the summer—hasn't stood for Kaddish during minyan all year."

This too was upsetting Shuli, absolutely.

"But he's twelve, yes?"

"Yes," Shuli says.

"Then that last one is not a worry. A boy, not yet a bar mitzvah, doesn't need to say Kaddish. He's sinless. There is no *aveirah* there."

"But reciting Kaddish is the highest praise to God that one can make," Shuli says. "Even if a child were a sinner and did nothing more than answer to the *y'hei sh'meih rabba*, he'd get a ticket into Heaven for that alone."

Miri considers, and Shuli isn't sure if she's doing it to be polite, pretending for her husband that she doesn't have her answer at the ready.

"And right there is the irony," is what she says. "Children aren't obligated to do anything, even if we leave them something as important as the Kaddish to recite. The *Shulchan Aruch* goes as far as saying that even though the Kaddish aids the departed in Heaven, it's far more important that a child walk in the path of righteousness than utter those words."

Shuli thinks this over, hugging his pillow. He says, "So Gavriel does nothing wrong."

"Can we talk about what this really is and isn't about, my husband?"

"Yes," Shuli says, his voice breaking.

"That boy is not you," Miri says. "You did your *t'shuvah* long ago. For how many years since do you light a candle on your father's *yahrzeit*? For how many do you stand for the Kaddish, putting forth your whole soul?" Miri leans her head on Shuli's shoulder. "Your whole soul for his."

Shuli turns and hugs her, burying his face in her neck.

"This boy at twelve is not you back when you were thirty, stoned and lazy, and wasting a life in advertising—"

"Branding," Shuli says, lifting his head and wiping his nose on the sleeve of his pajamas. "It's part of advertising. But branding is its own thing."

"The point is," she says, "you spending your days selling junk, and your nights trying to catch an STD to bring to this marriage, was necessary at the time. You needed to run away from yourself, to run from the obligations that you've since taken on, so that you might achieve ten times—no, a hundred times!— more than what you might ever have done without leaving. We should all be thankful that you, for so long, strayed."

IX

AT THE FIRST OF THE SPECIAL RECESSES, REB SHULI AND Gavriel sit as they had the day before, facing the Gemara on the same side of the desk, with Shuli's finger pressed to the commentary they're meant to learn. He doesn't begin teaching, instead launching back into their conversation as if not an instant has gone by.

"Why don't you stand in davening, sweet child?" Shuli asks. "Why don't you stand for the Kaddish?"

"I do," Gavriel says.

"You do?"

"Sometimes at night. For *Maariv*. With my brothers."

"With a minyan?"

The boy answers matter-of-factly. "You can't say it without."

"But at school? Why not here? There must be a reason."

And Shuli hears it in his own voice, the agitation—revealing an upset he didn't mean to share.

As if swapping roles, as if Gavriel is suddenly concerned only with alleviating Reb Shuli's unease, he says, "You want to know if I'm acting bad on purpose?"

"Yes. That's what I was trying to find out. If maybe you do what you do out of anger. Or if for some other reason. Because with rebellion, it can also be a way to acknowledge the importance of the thing we rebel against." Reb Shuli stops himself there, but Gavriel doesn't respond.

"What I'm trying to say is, sometimes the rejection is a way to let people know that the thing we reject truly matters. It is its own kind of faith, even if it's the opposite of faith."

Gavriel perks up. "You're saying it's OK if I don't eat kosher? Because the candy, I also snuck some home. There's more."

Shuli lets out an "Oy" that makes the boy blush.

"No. It's not OK to eat *treif.* And if you do, why bring it into your mother's kosher home?" Reb Shuli rubs his face with both hands and starts again. "Listen. It's a mature thing I'm going to tell you. Because I know that somewhere in there is a very mature young man. So let me ask you, do you know what is *kadosh*— what it means?"

"Holy," Gavriel answers.

"Yes, holy. Exactly. But the root of the word, it can also be used in the opposite way. In the Torah, in the book of *B'reishit,* our father Yehuda is looking for someone—I won't say who, because why spread such an accusation, even now. Yehuda asks if anyone has seen this certain woman, this *'kadeshah'* is what he says—meaning a prostitute. The same letters used to make up 'holy' are also used for the opposite of what is holy."

Reb Shuli has read that line in the Bible ten thousand times, pondering the roots of words, and of actions, their malleable meanings. He wants this half-orphan to understand that Shuli's own bitter misdeeds, fierce as they were, came from a place not of enmity but of deep, deep love.

He wants Gavriel to know he'd sat through his own father's mourning because of his upside-down devotion. And twenty years later, he wishes desperately that he could un-sit and do right. That is the warning he wants to share. To say, You'll never be able to pray all those prayers unuttered.

And yet, Reb Shuli is still too ashamed to admit to being the man he once was.

What he says instead is, "I want to know if you sit because you're mad."

"At my father?"

"Yes. For dying."

"I don't understand," the boy says. "Because it's his fault?"

Reb Shuli can see Gavriel's bottom lip beginning to wobble.

"No, no, no. *Chas v'chalilah.* God forbid. That's not what I meant. I just thought—"

"My mother," Gavriel says. "I'm mad at her."

Again, the boy's tone—it's as if he speaks out of pity for the suffering of his teacher.

"But why?" Reb Shuli says. "What has she done?"

"She broke a promise. She lied."

"I'm sure your mother didn't lie."

Gavriel looks back over his shoulder at the clock.

"Is it second recess yet?"

"No. It's still first recess. Anyway, there is only ever one recess. I made up the others so we could talk until we're done."

"What if it takes longer?"

"So I'll make more. A fourth and a fifth recess, even—only for you. Or for you and someone you pick to play with."

"You promise?"

"*Bli neder,* if it takes that long, then yes."

Gavriel, sharp child, says, "If I just tell you quick, can I have the fifth recess as the fourth?"

"You mean an extra for you and a friend?"

"Yes."

"If you tell me quick-quick, and if you and the friend play in the library and not the schoolyard, so I don't have to answer to the *rosh yeshiva* if he sees. You can have both fourth and fifth as a private recess for you and this friend."

Gavriel nods.

"When my father died, my mother promised I could choose anything of his that I wanted. That the youngest gets first pick."

"OK," Reb Shuli says.

"When I chose, she said no."

"That's not necessarily lying," Reb Shuli says, full of affection. "Not everything is for a child. Let's say he had a gun in his drawer."

"It wasn't a gun."

"I didn't think it was. I meant if you wanted a car that you couldn't drive, a better example."

"It was his Kiddush cup."

This sets a heavy silence over them both. It blocks out the noise from the playground, and the dull hiss from the PA system that never, in that classroom, seems to turn off.

"You wanted your father's Kiddush cup?"

"And my mother said no."

"Maybe because you're still a family, under one roof. Maybe while she's lucky enough to have you and your siblings at home, if there are others . . ."

"Leib. He's still home. And one of my sisters."

"See? That makes perfect sense. There's no reason to be mad. She wants it to stay. The family cup."

"She already gave it to Yisroel. It's at his house."

Reb Shuli does his best not to show it, but he has to admit, it does sound like a lie.

Gavriel then crosses his arms and presses that mouth closed.

This is when Shuli wishes he were better trained. He isn't a social worker, or even a licensed teacher, for that matter—you don't need some piece of paper from the state to teach Gemara in private school.

Shuli isn't quite sure if another bribe is, for the boy, good or bad. He assesses the situation as best he can and does what he needs to do.

"The triple recess today," Shuli says. "And a double tomorrow, for you and one friend."

"The Kiddush cup," Gavriel says. "It has our last name on the side. On the bottom, it says 1856. It's been used by our family for like two hundred years. My father made Kiddush with it every week."

"A treasure," Reb Shuli says, feeling stupid, as the treasure is already lost.

"My mother said that my father said that it was really important to him that it keep getting used every *Shabbos*, long after he was gone."

"This is what ritual does. It binds from chaos. Across time."

Reb Shuli asks if what he just said makes clear sense, and Gavriel gives his teacher a thumbs-up.

Then the boy says, "Me always being in trouble? With you, in here?"

"Yes?" Shuli answers, solemn.

"At home it's kind of always the situation. Even from before my dad. The *treif* candy. The money from the purse. I'm always getting punished for that kind of stuff—when I get caught. That's what she was saying, why I couldn't have it."

"What are you telling me?"

"Of the five of us kids, my mother says I'm the one who, if I don't fix it, will end up off the *derech*. Who'll end up not being *shomer Shabbos*, and not religious, and living like a goy."

"God forbid!" Reb Shuli says.

"She gave her word to my father that the cup would get used. That's what she told me. She said, even though she knows she made me a promise, she already made my father a bigger promise, and that one needed to be honored more, because he was the father, and because he was dead. So she couldn't, with a good heart, trust the cup to go to me. Considering how I act, is what she said. Then she told me to pick something else."

What to say now? How to build trust here, but not break it at home?

"She did this, your mother," Reb Shuli says, "because you might not, at some future time, do what a Jewish boy should?"

Gavriel nods.

"I'm sure your mother means well. But I want you to know, I believe, with all my heart, that you—you're a good boy. And I want you to know," Reb Shuli says, "if I didn't have children of my own, I'd give you my own Kiddush cup, believing it would be in the best of hands."

Shuli smiles down upon his student, who looks like he might cry. Then, Shuli sees, it's a different expression completely.

"Can I go to recess now?"

"Go," Reb Shuli says. "Play nice."

X

HOW OFTEN DOES MIRI STEER HIM IN THE RIGHT DIREC-
tion? How often does she know what's right? They bring
the children to the wedding, and it is, for Shuli, a true tonic for
the spirit.

At the *bedekken*, the bride sits stunning in a throne of a chair.
Putting aside his rabbinical duties, Shuli hooks Hayim's arm in
a joyous father-son moment, as they join the other men to dance
the *chassan* over, stomping and hooting, so that the groom may
veil his bride.

He spies Miri among the crowd of women, with Nava pulled
to her chest. His beautiful wife, her arms wrapped around their
daughter, winks at him when he nears.

Shuli celebrates at every step, *kiddushin* and *nissuin*, dinner
and dance. He swirls in every circle, singing along to every song.
When bride and groom are seated, Shuli is first to do a solo jig
before them and quick to grab the back of the groom's chair
when it's time to lift the couple into the air.

With the newlyweds hoisted above everyone's heads, someone grabs a napkin, so that the *chassan* can hold one corner and

the *kallah* the other. The heavy lifters raise and lower those chairs to the music, while new husband and wife howl, aloft.

Shuli stares up, admiring the union he'd just consecrated and which he very literally supports. The sweat stings his eyes, as he shoulders his burden.

And it's the thought of burdens and of unions, the idea of hoisting this couple toward Heaven, and the tension on the napkin they hold, that brings Shuli back to the signing of the *ketubah*. It has him contemplating the wedding contract, and the handkerchief the groom had given to Shuli to pass on to the *eidim*, the two kosher witnesses. It was a *kinyan* made to seal the deal, to represent physically the commitment entered into.

The realization hits Shuli so hard it nearly knocks him from his feet. He stumbles, weak kneed. The others, supporting the chair, shore it up in a panic. They stare at Shuli with a mix of concern and anger—fighting not to drop the *chassan* and spill him, like Humpty Dumpty, to the floor.

The chairs are hurriedly lowered, everyone grinning and clapping to cover it up, while Shuli stumbles off, past his son and daughter, and out of the hall. He can see Miri breaking away from the women's hora, as he heads toward the exit.

WHAT HAS LEFT SHULI LIGHT-HEADED IS THE UNDERSTANDing that all his years of *t'shuvah*, a lifetime of redemption, had—for his father—done nothing. Not the *yahrzeit* candles lit, nor the services led. It was twenty years of Kaddishes without meaning, as they were not Shuli's to say.

So maybe Gavriel doesn't stand when he should, but hadn't he sought a responsibility more lasting? Hadn't he gone after the legacy of his father's Kiddush cup, while well aware that his *yetzer hara*—his own budding evil inclination—would make owning it, for him, a great challenge?

This *pisher*, too young to grow even a wisp of beard, had succeeded where Shuli had failed. He'd tried to serve his father across time.

Shuli hasn't even made it to the end of the street before Miri catches up.

"What's gotten into you, husband?" she says, sincerely concerned. "Are you drunk? You look green."

"I've figured it out," he says. "What that boy has woken up in me."

"Not that student," Miri says, disappointed. "That's not what you're thinking about here."

"What better place," he says, "when overseeing contracts, when transforming love into law. It's the *kinyan*," Shuli tells her, looking around nervously, as if someone might overhear. "Just because I returned to the fold doesn't mean I brought everything back with me. On that website, a lifetime ago, I gave up what was mine."

"This isn't news, Shuli. How many times have we discussed this over the years? You paid for a service, and that's all."

"But it's not all. I don't know if I ever told you. When I signed, there was a digital pen that I put into a digital hand. I made a *kinyan*. I transferred over my rights—for real. Which means, even now, remembering my father is that other man's job."

"You're serious?" she says, and Shuli is. "You think that would hold up in a rabbinical court? A *shaliach mitzvah*, a representative acquiring that license in perpetuity? It wouldn't stand.

The passing of the pen, it's for optics, just for show. A wedding *kinyan* is a different deal."

"You always have the answers, my brilliant wife. But you don't know how a *beis din* would judge when it was my intent to be rid of that responsibility for life. The privilege doesn't just revert on its own. The other party would need to return it." And here Shuli thinks he might faint. "What if he wants to keep what he's been given? Where will I be then?"

"And how would you even find him to ask? But let me think about it," Miri says. "I can look it up. I can advise."

"I can tell you right where to look, Miri. In the Torah. At Avraham's death. The first Jewish father buried, and his two sons left to mourn. You can study that monster Esav, the firstborn, who traded his birthright for a bowl of lentils. Do you know what is written?"

"I do."

"But do you know what word specifically is used?"

"*Vayivez,*" Miri says.

"Yes, *vayivez*. To despise! Esav didn't just reject, he didn't just turn down, he purposely threw away his birthright because he despised it. This is the rot he and I both hold in our hearts."

"Oh, husband," Miri says, looking fully forlorn.

"Take the kids home," he says, already walking in the direction of school.

"What do I tell everyone?"

"That I'm sick. That I'm not well. Tell them it's mental indigestion. A little reflux of the soul."

XI

SHULI HURRIES ALONG, MUMBLING TO HIMSELF IN THE dark and following the rhythm of his thoughts . . . *Kiddush, Kaddish, kadosh, kadeshah.* He rolls that loaded root around in his noggin, tracking it from sacred to profane.

It's almost a relief to discover the truth of his empty redemption, to uncover—through Gavriel, of all people—that Shuli was living a ghost life, a spiritual existence that one could, like steam, push a finger through.

All the years of teaching and outreach, all the effort dedicated to *t'shuvah,* it was as if he'd been saving money for twenty years only to find he'd been depositing it into someone else's account. Regarding the one thing that mattered to Shuli, the very spark that started the fire of his rebirth, the Kaddish still belonged to Chemi, who roamed as true heir, Shuli's dead father's legal son.

Rushing toward the yeshiva, distractedly crossing against the light, a skateboarder nearly hits him, jumping from his board, which clatters past. The young man somehow sticks the landing, coming to a halt.

Shuli picks up the board, which is a beauty. A perfect fit for a skater whose costume is as complete as Shuli's own, from his baseball hat down to his sneakers. Shuli can see in the skater's gaze how he is being seen, with his long beard and black hat, and the fancy silk *bekishe* he wears for weddings. How easy it is to fool people with one's outside, even if the work hasn't been done within.

"Nice deck," Shuli says, passing the skateboard back.

"Thanks," the man says, skating off. Shuli considers calling after him, asking to use his phone.

Such a temptation as a cell phone with Internet, Shuli didn't allow for himself or his family. There was no Wi-Fi in their house. No laptops or desktops. Such a portal to temptation isn't safe when the children are small, and is even more dangerous as they turn big, which is why he races to the computer room at school.

Just thinking about logging on musters the image Shuli has involuntarily pictured countless times. There it is, that poor woman and her glass dildo, taking form in his mind's eye.

Shuli's father had warned him against the permanence of a tattoo, but this, this is even worse. How it haunts him. "Dildo!" Shuli thinks. That he even still knows the word is pure wretchedness. He picks up his pace, as if he might leave that memory behind.

BEFORE HEADING INTO THE COMPUTER ROOM, REB SHULI runs to the teachers' lounge for the corkboard he'd hung over his shared desk. Pinned to it were flyers for this and that, the new class schedules tacked above the old. In pride of place were the photographs of former students at different milestones and, blessedly, those students' children—some of whom would soon enough be in Shuli's class. Buried beneath it all, the very first thing he'd affixed to that blank board was the picture of Chemi, leaning over a book.

Reb Shuli stands there with the moon cutting grayly through the sad unwashed window, feeling blessed with clarity and a vision for repair. He lifts that corkboard from its hook on the wall and rests it flat on his desk. Shuli begins pulling tacks and tossing papers. It is, for Reb Shuli, like peeling back time. Layer after layer, year after year.

XII

R EB SHULI SITS IN FRONT OF A SPACE-AGE MONITOR IN
the computer room, searching for its base. He can't find
the cord that runs from the monitor to the tower, or, for that
matter, the tower itself. On top of it all—this was something—
the keyboard and mouse lie untethered, cut loose.

It's no short stretch before Reb Shuli understands that the
computer, the guts of it, are built into that sliver of a screen.
The whole machine was pressed into that sleek, flat space.

After some fiddling, Reb Shuli finds the button to turn the
accursed thing on. He feels a quick rush of pride when, guessing
at icons, he finds himself on the World Wide Web. Years away
from all this nonsense, and he'd managed to figure it out.

Such shrewdness only confirmed what he'd always been
taught. If one is well versed in the Torah, all other knowledge
will be yours.

This time, Reb Shuli knows exactly what to enter. He
looks at his picture of Chemi, takes a deep breath, and types
in kaddish.com.

He's whisked to the site with a speed he couldn't have imagined. There it is, still active, still providing its miraculous service to the shirkers and deadbeats of the world.

How far the site has come from that fish-mouthed dawn at his sister's house. The design is as streamlined and space-aged as the machine on which he views it. Across the top of the page runs a banner with a number that looks as if it's actually printed in bronze, so dimensional and solid does it appear.

What Reb Shuli can't fathom is what he sees written there. The number reads, "2,784." Below it, in that same hefty type, it says "souls served."

And just like that, while he's watching and absorbing, the last digit turns, right before his eyes, from a four to a five.

He looks at his watch. Barely dawn in Israel, and these fine men hard at work, engaged in their monkish labors.

In the center of that home page, lovely pictures of the students studying and praying rotate in a well-choreographed cascade. Reb Shuli stares at them, misty, with his pinpricked and faded photo of Chemi set alongside the keyboard.

He watches this new generation of *talmidei chachamim*, mesmerized and wondering if his ancient image of Chemi might materialize.

When he's sat through the complete slide show what must have been a dozen times, feeling moved, feeling connected to that distant study hall, he tours the other tabs.

Everything one might want to familiarize oneself with the service, to be made comfortable and secure in the application process, Reb Shuli locates with ease. The single thing he has trouble tracking down is the single thing he's after. He's looking for a contact page where he might call or write someone directly.

It's been eons since Reb Shuli needed information that an old copy of the yellow pages, or a favor asked of Mrs. Meyers, the school secretary, could not help him find. How helpless he feels, searching fruitlessly for a place to write a letter to the manager, or the webmaster, or whatever the word, today, was.

Reb Shuli tries to stay positive, imagining himself sitting across a table from a middle-aged Chemi, explaining who he'd been then and who he was now. He'd offer thanks to Chemi for being his emancipator—the one who'd freed him from his obligations. And that's the rub, is what Shuli would say, for now Chemi had inadvertently become his captor, the one who keeps him shackled to his old ungrateful self.

He would then broach a reverse *kinyan*. Let Chemi pass off something symbolic, maybe an actual pen after all this time, and then let Shuli reclaim his mantle so that he might raise his own head high—if only to look Chemi in the eye in this world, and his father in the next.

When summoned to the World to Come, Shuli wants nothing more than to take his seat at that infinite table with dignity, to learn Torah unencumbered by time.

He clicks and clicks and clicks. Getting nowhere, Shuli navigates his way back to that opening page. What he finds truly amazes. Had it been five minutes? Ten? And the number had already gone up once more: 2,786.

SHULI GOES HOME TO HIS FAMILY AND SLEEPS A DEEP SLEEP, hugging his Miri until morning. He walks to school with a spring in his step, not at all put off by his failure to make contact, excited only for the journey ahead.

He waves to the students as they hop off buses and sprout

from the subway entrances. He waits on the yeshiva's front steps, taking it in, watching the walkers walk and the well-to-do exit their Ubers. He drinks in all that youthful energy as the future of the Jewish people piles through the school's front doors.

The bells have yet to ring, and davening is still a few minutes off. Shuli fetches his coffee and drinks it in front of the same computer he'd used the night before. He's already come up with a solution. Shuli returns to the site and clicks on the introductory form.

He enters his name, and where he's asked for the name of the deceased, he puts "G-d Forbid It Should Be So" as a first name and "All Are Well, Tfu, Tfu, Tfu" as a last.

Where biographical details are requested, he types a simple, friendly note—Chemi-style. He wishes he'd kept that long-lost one-line letter he'd received.

Reb Shuli writes only "I'm trying to locate a student named Chemi who prayed on my father's behalf, and in my stead. With Care, Shuli." He leaves, as a contact, the school e-mail address that Mrs. Meyers checks for him, and from which she prints out the parents' e-mails when they write, and into which she types Shuli's handwritten responses when a phone call won't do.

With the form submitted, Reb Shuli races for his tallis bag and slips into davening. There he rocks at his *shtender,* keeping the boys focused, making sure their lips are moving and, with his renegades, giving a faux-supportive squeeze to the shoulder, to check if their tzitzit are on under their shirts.

When the Kaddish comes and he sees Gavriel sitting silent, it puts an ache in Shuli's heart.

During the breakfast break, Reb Shuli hovers around Mrs. Meyers's desk, though she's told him his in-box is empty.

He teaches a double period of Gemara, sneaking over at the start and end of recess, and, once, pretending he needed to use the bathroom so that he might pass the anteroom outside the *rosh yeshiva*'s office, where Mrs. Meyers sits.

To his query, he receives no reply.

He checks with Mrs. Meyers during lunch, asking her to refresh and refresh and refresh. He does the same around *Minchah*, stopping by on the way to, and from, afternoon prayers.

He returns again at the end of classes. Mrs. Meyers pulls on her coat very obviously, and ties her scarf with a sort of anger, trying with every movement to signal that her day is done.

What Mrs. Meyers has already recognized, what Reb Shuli is only beginning to face, is the exhibition of a kind of behavior from Reb Shuli that Reb Shuli thought he'd long ago conquered. His anticipation over locating Chemi, of seeing his sonly duties restored—it is extraordinarily, relentlessly consuming.

Standing alone in the empty hallway, with Mrs. Meyers gone, Shuli can't stop agonizing over when his reply might come. That this obsessive streak is so easily triggered in him leaves Shuli breathless with fear.

ON THE SECOND DAY OF WAITING, HE FIGHTS BOTHERING that nice woman with all his might—allowing himself only a polite morning and evening query. Shuli doesn't sleep that night.

On the third day of racked anticipation, the day the Bible makes clear is the apex for any kind of hurt, Reb Shuli shuffles into Mrs. Meyers's office, approaching with greatest humility, his eyes cast down.

So low does he stare that his view is of the dinged and dented metal legs to Mrs. Meyers's desk, and the near colorless industrial tile on which they rest. What he does not see is that Mrs. Meyers, expecting him, already holds out a piece of paper.

As he accepts it, Mrs. Meyers does something Reb Shuli has never seen before. She rolls her eyes. Just as his sister would. A near-perfect match.

"Thank you," he says, though he's not at all thankful. He can already tell it's not his dreamed-of reply—a disappointment that so rattles Shuli, the paper shakes in his hand. Instead of a letter, Mrs. Meyers has given him instructions for the school's e-mail system. In thick black marker she's added his e-mail address (which he knows) and his password (which he purposefully doesn't).

"You're on your own," she says. "The e-mail Pony Express is hereby out of business. I'm shooting the horse."

"Understood," Reb Shuli says, trying to sound chipper, while the fear already gripping him twists tight.

He hadn't planned to let a computer back into his life. The surfing he'd done, the form he'd sent, he'd intended it to be a singular, outlying occasion. It was, Shuli had hoped and prayed, a onetime affair.

XIII

FORBIDDEN FROM HOUNDING MRS. MEYERS, REB SHULI finds himself again bedeviled by the machines. He can't keep himself from the computer room, or off the computer. He's there at the start and end of davening every morning, and at every period break. In the days that follow, he leaves his own class more than once to interrupt another. He waves at the computer teacher, saying, "Go on, go on," as he sits down at an empty workstation to check his e-mail again.

Shuli can't rid himself of the sense that he'd entered his address wrong and that he, not Chemi, was the one who couldn't be reached. He can't fathom any other explanation for the silence, which is why, each morning, Reb Shuli submits the same form again.

It's a theory he clings to until he's faced that empty in-box for the whole of a week. That's when he decides his terseness must be at fault. He's clearly coming off as too cold and too remote, and so he begins sending long epistolary meditations about his father and Chemi, about his wife and precious children, about all he'd done wrong in the past, and those things he now does right.

He fires off mini-musings like, "Do you know how old my father seemed when I lost him? Only at fifty do I see how young a man he really was."

Shuli hopes that whoever is receiving these dispatches might take pity and reply. In the interim, he begins searching for another way to make contact on his own.

Luddite that he is, Shuli still knows how to poke around the Internet, googling different permutations of the bits of information he has. Beyond some happy Yelp reviews, Shuli can't find anything concrete, no direct e-mail or phone number or Jerusalem address, leaving him feeling as if he might actually lose his mind. What if he never finds anyone? What if he does—but they tell him Chemi has disappeared? What if, in that volatile region, some tragedy, God forbid, has struck Chemi and it's too late to put what was so egregiously wrong into the right?

What if someone this very minute mourns his mourner?

With this new worry, Shuli begins writing the site with panicked missives, inquiring about Chemi's health and well-being, and pleading for news.

Often, after hitting send, he berates himself for coming off as too intrusive or too hysterical, and so follows up with apologies, which he immediately regrets sending, and which also garner no reply.

Two weeks in, and Shuli can't take it any longer. He is in the gym that doubles as a lunchroom that triples as a house of prayer. He crosses his eyes, and straightens the box of his tefillin on his head and adjusts the wings of his tallis on his back. Abandoning his lectern, Shuli slides onto a bench, alongside some pious, dutiful boys. He stares mournfully at the basketball hoop hanging above him, wondering how he might face another day. He imagines himself seated across from Chemi. In his daydream, that gym humming with prayer transforms into a little *steakiyah* in Jerusalem, with him and Chemi at a table for two, a bowl of hummus and a plate of fresh pita between them.

The true distance from that reality so saddens Reb Shuli, he lets out an audible sigh. All the boys look his way but for Gavriel, daydreaming himself, his head tilted back and his eyes glazed with wonder.

Why hadn't Shuli thought of it until now? The solution is obvious. Those same lost students who didn't know their way around a page of Gemara were also the ones who could, blindfolded, build a cell phone from loose parts. In this world, the one in which we're forced to plod miserably along, these boys cared for nothing. But in the alternate universe of computers and games, these monsters shined. Gavriel could surely help him out.

It was a Friday, a short day, when the kids go home early to prepare for *Shabbat*. Reb Shuli, who knows he can't corral the child until after the weekend, spends his own *Shabbos* preparations stiff with anticipatory stress.

Miri, who has nearly given up on him, who has begged him to seek from his own rabbi some advice, now presses him to make an appointment with their psychiatrist neighbor.

"To mope around in front of the children, when the *Shabbat Malkah* is about to descend, it doesn't make sense," Miri says, referring to the Sabbath Queen that alights on every Jewish home. "And it doesn't make sense to suffer like this over a Kaddish for a father twenty years in the ground."

Shuli follows the words, doing his best to signal serious concern.

"Are you listening to me?" Miri says. "On *Shabbos*, even the dead are given a break from the tortures of Hell. I'm worried for your health." She taps at her temple, letting him know where the problem rests, and tells him to go knock on their neighbor's door and at least ask for a few pills. "You're in a depression, Shuli. A real one. I think it's a delayed kind of trauma over your father, coming to catch you two decades late."

"Sadness," Shuli says, "doesn't hide away for that long."

"It absolutely does. If this house had Internet, I'd show you."

"Not that discussion now, I'm begging," he says.

"So forget the computer and trust your wife! Your student has stirred everything up. Maybe that's a blessing. Because now you can face it and let it go. Gavriel is the one to tip you over, but I've watched, for too long, as you teeter on the edge."

"I'm not crazy," Shuli yells. "And I'm not teetering or tipping or depressed."

"Super-duper! Then prove it. Sleep when it's time to sleep, and be happy when you're awake."

"I will."

"If you don't, it's the doctor. Make a real appointment and start on some pills. It's your choice, but you need some peace, either way. Choke it down with water, or find it in your heart."

Shuli opts for the latter. He tries to muster all weekend, picturing himself with Chemi, the two of them walking a street in Jerusalem, chatting and holding hands. He flashes an overly broad, strained smile whenever Miri glances his way.

ON MONDAY, SHULI WAITS INSIDE THE SCHOOL'S FRONT door for Gavriel to arrive. As soon as the boy walks in, Shuli rushes over and gives a good squeeze to his shoulder, friendly.

But the boy looks bitter. He pulls the tassels of his tzitzit from under his shirt and says, "I'm wearing them. They're already on!"

"No, no, *chas v'chalilah,*" Reb Shuli says. "I wasn't checking. God forbid! I only wanted to let you know that you've really been, these days, toeing the line in class. As a thank-you, I'm instituting a triple recess today—in your honor."

Gavriel just stares.

"For being a good boy. A tribute!"

"Do I have to talk to you again?"

"During recess? No. You'll be outside, with the others. Otherwise it wouldn't be a treat. What I could use is some help now, before davening."

Shuli can see the child wondering if it's some sort of trap.

"Do you remember when I said we were in some ways the same?"

"Because our fathers are dead?"

"Yes," Shuli says. "But in some ways, we're very different. In those ways—with what I need help with—you're better and smarter, for sure."

THEY SIT SIDE BY SIDE IN THE EMPTY COMPUTER ROOM. AS a joke, to warm things up, Reb Shuli says, "If I'm the student, and you're the teacher, you should at least get the hat." And he drops his fine black fedora on the boy's head.

With the home page open, Shuli explains that he's trying to find someone who worked for the site, "an old friend," and that he's been filling out the form but nothing comes back.

"Maybe you can help me find an electronic contact or a P.O. box at some post office, where I can send an actual note."

The boy shrugs and starts typing. He slides his chair away from Shuli, who is crowding him, so Shuli stands and paces the room. Shuli bites his nails, wondering at the ethics of keeping a child away from the prayers he anyway ignores. And what if the boy tattles about this? Already, Shuli's crazy, made-up notion of the "triple recess" was being demanded by students in other grades.

"Is there anything?" Shuli asks, when the *click-clacking* stops.

"Nothing," Gavriel says.

"But you're good at this, yes?"

"I'm OK. There's a kid in Reb Yellin's class who knows how to write code. I could go get him."

"No, no. You're my expert. Keep doing what you're doing. Try some more."

Reb Shuli posts himself at the window, looking down onto the playground. It's absurd that these Jerusalem scholars engage in the intimate, subscriber-based work that they do and make it so hard to be found. Where was the customer service?

Again Gavriel stops, and when Shuli looks over, the boy tilts that black hat back at a rakish angle, though it's ten sizes too big.

"On a regular site, there's always a contact page, or a place with a little envelope, or phone, to click on. You know, a widget?"

Reb Shuli shakes his head. He does not know from widgets.

"I'm saying, there are sites where it's easy to find, and sites where it's hard. But on this one, it just isn't."

Reb Shuli stands there, bewildered, and Gavriel frowns.

"If a website has no address and no phone number," Gavriel

says, "if the domain owner is hidden on GoDaddy or whoever's hosting, and there's nowhere to write on kaddish.com except that application page, I'm saying, whoever's running it, do you think they want to be found?"

Reb Shuli concentrates deeply, mulling over what he's just heard. At the same time, he absorbs this new version of Gavriel, competent and well spoken, this surprising, complicated child, who has—Reb Shuli can't believe it—just made everything clear.

"Stay here!" Reb Shuli says, practically running from the room, like a child himself.

He returns with a *masechta* of Talmud, flipping through pages as he walks through the door. Yes, the wonders of schooling, every interaction offers the opportunity both to teach and to learn.

Shuli again sits next to Gavriel, leafing through the tractate of *Yoma,* until he gets to the second side of page *lamed-chet.* "Here," he says, happily. "Here is where we learn about the people on whose shoulders Earth rests. It's from the virtue of one righteous man alone that God may grant us all—every moving, breathing thing—the right to live on. It's said of Reb Shimon that no rainbow ever appeared during the whole of his lifetime, for we were—all of us—considered to be huddled under the arch of his goodness."

The boy appears confused and unsettled, the same as in class. But in this case, Shuli can tell that he's honestly trying to absorb.

"I'm trying to tell you," Reb Shuli says, "that I was wasting my time wondering why I couldn't find a certain person. Then you, my star pupil, lay bare the reason. It's so simple! Maybe the man doesn't want to be found."

Inspired, Reb Shuli says, "Can I trust you further?"

Gavriel says he can.

Reb Shuli explains the very bad choices he'd made as a young man, telling Gavriel about his lost years, and the shivah at his sister's, and—skipping the part that shames him—about his *kinyan* and the workings of the kaddish.com site. He lays it out in detail, while running his fingers over that passage in the Gemara, as if the words had suddenly risen up and could be felt like braille.

"These selfless individuals at kaddish.com are tzaddikim. We are dealing with the righteous of the righteous, busy with their holy job. They want no thanks, no praise, no accolades of any kind. Nothing beyond fair payment—which makes it even more kosher—while they perform the work that they do in the name of God."

"OK," Gavriel says.

"It's more than OK. It's a relief," Shuli says, absolutely beaming. "Do you know what is another word for 'tzaddikim'?"

"In Hebrew?" the boy asks, though he very obviously has no answer to give.

"The word," Shuli says, "is *nastirim*. From *l'hastir*, to hide. They, the *nastirim*, are the hidden ones. The man I look for has made himself invisible in his modesty."

"So you don't need to find him anymore?"

"*L'hefech!*" And Reb Shuli, playful, puts a hand atop the crown of the hat on Gavriel's head. He presses it down, until the boy's ears bend under the brim. "It's the opposite. Now that I know he strives to live quietly among us, I understand that I must redouble my efforts if I'm ever to obtain what is rightfully mine."

XIV

A T LUNCHTIME, REB SHULI SITS AT THE SAME TERMINAL with the book of *Vayikra* open and propped up against the screen. He looks to Moses to better apprehend what drives the meek to answer a call, spurred on by the morning's advance.

He's starting to get nervous, when Gavriel comes through the door, dragging his feet and eating a peanut butter sandwich.

"Did you find the boy from Yellin's *shiur*?" Shuli says.

"He's an eleventh grader. He pushed me into a locker and was going to close it. Then I told him a teacher sent me—but without giving a name."

"Good, good. What did he say?"

"He said if you used them before and they wrote back, why not reply to the old e-mail?"

Reb Shuli lets out a snort, full of disgust. "Children!" he says. "None of you can imagine what it's like for time to go by. Do you know how long ago 1999 is in computer years? Do you even know what is Eudora or WorldCom?"

"No."

"How about MindSpring or MCI?"

"My grandmother uses BellSouth for e-mail. Is it that?"

"Businesses come and go. Fashions change. If I still had the account, I'd already have pulled up the letter and hit send."

"OK," Gavriel says. "He said to tell you that first, just in case."

"Well, it's not the case."

"So then it's about finding the ISP."

Here it begins, Reb Shuli thinks, preparing for the barrage of acronyms whose meanings Reb Shuli can't even begin to guess at, all the *roshei tevot* of the modern world.

"What is ISP?"

"Well, not the ISP. That's the Internet Provider. But the ISP address. That's what I mean. The Internet is kind of everywhere all at once, like—" and Reb Shuli freezes, terrified the boy might compare the Internet to the Holy Spirit. What he says instead is "It's, like, just in the air. But to get onto it, if you want to interface—"

Gavriel pauses to see if his teacher is keeping up.

"Yes, yes," Shuli says. "I understand. 'Interface,' it's just a regular English word."

"You have to get onto it from somewhere. You know, from a physical place. Even if where you're surfing to is virtual."

"The information highway," Reb Shuli says. "Entrances and exits."

"So to zero a person. To find them. All you have to do is get someone from the site to write us back, but to our server."

Shuli raises up one of his giant eyebrows.

"This boy told you that?"

"Eitan did. That's his name. It's pretty simple. He says we need to put a GIF in an e-mail—just a tiny image, like the school logo—and if they answer, we get the IP address on our server and also the Lat Long. Which is just like it is on a map. It'll give us the computer's exact place. I don't even mean just the house. I mean what room it's in."

The way Gavriel explains it—the confidence radiating from the boy—it really makes a teacher proud. Reb Shuli is now hopeful not just about locating Chemi, but for a good and bright future for the child.

What he didn't understand was how they would get a reply to a second letter with the logo, if the righteous at kaddish.com were never going to answer the first. Shuli's face falls.

"Don't worry, Rebbe," Gavriel says. "I already know how I'm going to get them to write us. It's my idea," he says. "Not Eitan's."

"You think I don't know you're smart? Lazy is why I pick on you. Smart, I never doubted."

"Why not just pretend someone new is dead? Make up a person, and a new e-mail address. Act like you're hiring them for real."

"To invent a loss?" Shuli says. "It would be a lie. And, God help us, a sure way to court the evil eye."

"So let's use my father. He's already dead."

Reb Shuli's jaw drops at the inappropriate and unethical nature of Gavriel's proposal. It's a uniquely horrible way to employ the assistance of this child.

But Reb Shuli also recognizes its simple genius. He considers the idea, his mouth open, as if preparing to swallow Gavriel up.

Gavriel stares back at him, proud.

"I could bring in a picture of my dad. We can upload it as

the GIF if we get an answer, and if they write back one more time—"

"We get the ISP," Shuli says.

"And the Lat Long! So even if they're hiding from you . . ."

"We'll still know right where they are."

This child, every instant anew, proves cleverer to his teacher. So much so that Shuli turns to Gavriel not for technical advice but for actual wisdom, his defenses completely down.

"Isn't it spying?" Shuli asks, now worried over the thorny ethics of ferreting out the location of a yeshiva that wants to be hidden.

"It's just data. If you can get it, it's totally fair," Gavriel says. "Eitan's just showing us how to mine what's already there."

"It still feels a little like stealing," Reb Shuli says. "Can we maybe sleep on it first?"

"Whatever you want," Gavriel says. "I'm a kid. I have to come to school tomorrow either way."

THAT NIGHT, SHULI PUTS ON HIS PAJAMAS AND CLIMBS INTO bed. He closes his eyes and drapes a heavy arm around Miri. Like that, like a regular person, he drifts off to sleep.

At school the next morning, he waits for Gavriel on the building's front steps. He feels refreshed and well rested. Out of nowhere he remembers that he'd dreamt the loveliest dream of his own lost father. He takes this as a sign.

Up in the computer room, the two fill out the form together, with Gavriel answering the questions truthfully. In the field specified for anecdotal material, the boy shares a touching story about a father-son visit to the aquarium at Coney Island. It melts Shuli's heart.

When they're done, Gavriel reaches out and then stays his own hand, his finger hovering in the air.

"Do you want to do it?" he asks his teacher.

"No, you," Shuli says.

Gavriel presses the button, and the computer's speakers give off a satisfying whoosh.

BY AFTERNOON PRAYERS, AN ANSWER FROM THE SITE'S administrator is already waiting in Gavriel's account.

They find that they've been matched with not one but four different students, among whom they're invited to choose.

Each scholar has a different price attached based on years of learning, and, on top of that, different packages are available. The bereaved can sign up to have extra study dedicated to the deceased's memory, or have a *yahrzeit* candle lit for five, ten, fifteen years. . . .

It's all much more advanced, and expensive, than the program for which Reb Shuli—that is, Larry—had, so long ago, signed up.

Gavriel takes a passport-sized picture of his father out of his wallet and hands it to his teacher. Shuli scrutinizes the man in the photo, and then the snapshot itself—fresh and uncreased. What would it look like when this poor ragamuffin reached Shuli's age?

Gavriel takes the picture back and heads over to the scanner, while Shuli stands by the classroom door, his face pressed to the sliver of window, steaming it up and keeping an eye on the hallways, terrified another rabbi might stroll by.

It's no more than a minute before the boy is seated again, and another two before Gavriel is completely done.

"That's it?" Shuli says.

"I asked if we could pay by check and stuck in the GIF with my dad. If they write back, we're good."

XV

SHULI DOESN'T BOTHER TRYING TO SLEEP THAT NIGHT. HE lies next to Miri, attempting to calm himself off the rhythm of her breath. When that doesn't work, he tiptoes into each of the children's rooms to stand, as he has since they were born, at the end of their beds. Their peace, his peace.

He goes down to the kitchen and the terrible emptiness returns. Shuli puts on the kettle, opening the spout to keep it from whistling. He lugs a pile of holy books to the kitchen table. He eats half a babka over the sink and then digs into his studies with a mug of hot water and lemon, cooling.

Shuli doesn't search for a practical solution to end his suffering. That, he already has. He must reacquire what he'd squandered—he needed his birthright back. What he spends the night exploring is why such agony had been brought into his life.

Shuli happens upon the explanation in the Ramban's *Shaar HaGemul*, a monograph on death. Sometimes punishment is meted out to the living, not because of sin but because of a deficit of positive deeds. His misery was just the kind delivered to a son who sat idle in this world, while his own father was judged in the next.

Shuli leaves the house before anyone wakes and gets caught in the rain on the way to school. He arrives soaked through.

When Gavriel shows up to the computer room as ordered, he finds his teacher's clothing hung on the backs of the chairs. A tie on one. A jacket on the other. Even Shuli's dress shirt is off. His teacher stands barefoot in his drying suit pants, and with his undershirt and tzitzit wet and clinging to his chest.

Gavriel blinks but makes no comment, sitting down and signing on to his e-mail account. He finds not one but two letters waiting.

Shuli is far too anxious to read the e-mails himself, and asks Gavriel to tell him what they say.

The first, in response to Gavriel's fake inquiry, sends condolences for his loss and confirms again that someone would be available to start praying immediately upon receipt of payment, but unfortunately they couldn't accept a personal check. The second was an auto-reminder, letting Gavriel know that his credit card information had not been received. Both were signed "The kaddish.com Team."

"So, *nu?*" Shuli says, waiting for Gavriel to get working.

"I kind of need Eitan's help with this part."

"No help," Shuli says. "Just us. Go learn what to do, smart boy. Take him from davening to teach you, if need be."

"From davening?" Even naughty Gavriel can't believe it.

"*Pikuach nefesh,*" Reb Shuli says. "To save a life, all is permitted." And he does not go on to say that it's his own that hangs in the balance.

Gavriel runs off, leaving his rebbe to his pacing.

The boy returns with a spiral notebook, from which he works, following the instructions that Eitan has scribbled inside.

As Gavriel hunts for a physical address, Reb Shuli moves back and forth between the hallway window, which he nervously checks, and the street-side view, where he finally settles. He doesn't stare down at the playground but turns his gaze eastward, toward Jerusalem, the direction in which they pray.

When he first entered this miserable room and found his way back onto the Web, Shuli had prided himself on the belief that all knowledge was contained inside the Torah. And now, as he waits for Gavriel to pinpoint the exact spot on the planet where this hidden yeshiva stood, he's forced to admit that inside this terrible machine is a different kind of all-knowingness. A toxic, shiftless omniscience.

To unlock the secrets of the Torah, one had to be disciplined. One had to work and to think. But this? If one only knew how to ask the question, all knowledge was lazily yours.

Looking over at Gavriel, Shuli can remember being this boy's age, and the kinds of thoughts he'd had. He can recall sitting on the front stoop and watching his busy neighbors rushing by. Shuli would ponder what it meant for God to know where every living person was at any given moment, tracking what they were doing, what they were eating, their every action and urge. He'd count up all the people he could name, trying to hold them in his thoughts all at once, and, his head actually aching with the strain, Shuli would then picture those people multiplied again and again until they equaled every single person on Earth. Then he'd wonder what it would be like to keep up with the goings-on of all those beings, along with what they'd done before and what they were planning for the future—tabulating everything simultaneously in a singular Godlike mind.

And here in these machines is that exact knowing—for the advertisers and for the governments and for those with good and bad intentions to use as they saw fit. It's all accessible, your wants and dreams, your sins and secrets, so that Gavriel, tapping away at the keys, can tell where someone around the world sits right then—a humble, hidden someone who does not want to be found. But the Internet knows, and it has no compass to guide it and no will to guard what was meant only for the Maker. Here, it all waits to be plucked out of the air by a child.

Shuli's head aches from the thought, as it had back on that stoop. And so he does as he did back then. He closes his eyes and, palms to his cheeks, presses his fingers against their lids, pressing and pressing, until the darkness sends colors rushing toward him, as if he's hurtling through space. He stops only when he sees, like fireworks, beautiful glints of light.

In them, Shuli recognizes the source of it all. The flashes of pure energy firing through cables under the ocean, soaring up, and making their way to satellites turning in the heavens. All the world's understanding transformed into waves of light and sound, to modulated impulse and frequency, everyone's deepest desires broadcast in an ever-expanding and invisible net. He can feel them pulsing through his body, dappling the very air he breathes.

Gavriel cries out. He does so with the full force of a eureka moment, startling Reb Shuli from his reverie. He follows this with a happy sort of squeal and jumps from his chair. He runs to the window and excitedly, maybe even lovingly, grabs Shuli by his belt, pulling him back over to the machine.

A satellite picture of a neighborhood is pulled up, an image taken from the sky. It is, Reb Shuli can already tell, a section of the Holy City as seen from above. A God's-eye view of Jerusalem.

The boy clicks and clicks, zooming in. Shuli warms at the sight of those red rooftops, and the dusty gray ribbons of road. Yerushalyim rising up to meet him.

"Rebbe, it's here, the yeshiva," Gavriel says. "Eitan's thing. It really works."

Shuli wants to sound wise and to sound confident, but he can't seem to speak. He steps back from the computer, retreating toward his window.

"It's not right," Shuli says. "To see such a thing."

"It's a satellite picture. It's free. It's public!"

"Spying," Shuli says. "Sneaking around. Peeping into someone's life."

"We're not looking into their windows or anything. I mean, we sort of can. There's a street view. We can do a virtual walk-by."

"No," Shuli says, trying to process what the boy has just done, what Shuli has facilitated, horrified and exhilarated in equal measure. "Enough technology," he says. "Enough screens. Enough deception. We tricked them into making contact when they expressly wanted to be left to their labors. Write them back and tell them the truth. Do it now! A good lesson for teacher and student, both."

Gavriel looks crestfallen. He'd worked hard and succeeded. And now Shuli was telling him to throw it all away.

And what, Shuli thinks, does the boy see looking back? His pale, exhausted rebbe, practically in his *gatkes*—half naked, and clearly in pain. Yes, this must be what he sees, for Gavriel goes into his book bag for his pencil case. He takes out a highlighter and a marker and a pen. With that spiral notebook in his lap, he turns to a fresh page and begins to draw. Sounding like a grown man, he says to Shuli, "Look out your window, Rebbe. Take a rest."

Shuli frowns a happy, doting frown, accepting this advice.

He stares out the window, peering over the playground to the other side of the street. He cranes his neck trying to find a space between buildings, even an inch of horizon, so that he might stare across the six thousand miles, draw a bead on that computer in the Holy City, and on the man who sits in the glow of its screen.

"Can I show you what I've done?" Gavriel asks. "On paper, not the computer at all."

Without turning to face the boy, Reb Shuli politely declines. "I don't need to see anything. I don't want to know. If one has been treated honorably one should act so in return."

He then asks the boy to type an e-mail on his behalf and from his personal account. Shuli—no longer using Gavriel as a proxy—dictates the letter, while the boy hunts and pecks at the keys.

Shuli wants the fine folk at the yeshiva to know that he is sorry. And that he, and his student, Gavriel, both feel great appreciation for the wonderful options offered, but that the services of kaddish.com were, in actuality, not needed. Shuli asks that his own deceit be forgiven, and Gavriel's excused—for any fault was, as the responsible adult, wholly his own. There were extenuating circumstances that Shuli was hoping might be overlooked. Really, the whole ruse had been thought up to find a former scholar, surely long gone. Again, he only wants to make contact so that he might offer thanks and facilitate the return of something that was meant to be his. If the unseemly way they'd reached this point muddled things, Shuli hopes they might still believe that it is with deepest respect that such a request is being made.

That's the gist of the letter the two send off.

And it's the last they hear from kaddish.com.

XVI

I F THE PRIOR PERIOD OF SILENCE HAD BEEN TORTUROUS to Reb Shuli, this—an active rejection—fills him with an unrelenting despair. He barely survives until *Shabbos,* which is an unmitigated disaster.

Prohibited from touching electronics of any kind, Shuli feels his most Larry-like impulses emerging. By Saturday lunch, he's so distracted that he stumbles through the Kiddush. Holding that brimming cup high above the table, the children giggle as Shuli sloshes wine over the sides.

The urge to sneak into school to fiddle with that *mukzah* computer is so great, he actually asks Miri to restrain him. It's the closest he's come to breaking the Sabbath since he'd turned religious again.

Miri leads him out back after *benching* and sits him on the steps to their overgrown yard. She takes his hand between hers and holds it in her lap. "There," she says, "you're restrained."

He goes on to tell her everything he's done, filling her in on the control lost at school, the boundaries crossed. Miri hears it all with equanimity until he gets to the photo that he and Gavriel attached to their letter.

"Did you really use a picture of that poor boy's father, may his memory be blessed?"

Shuli tells her that he had. And just as Miri starts on being horrified, the children scramble out of the house. They lean on their parents' backs, hugging their necks—Nava on his, and Hayim on hers.

"Go nap," Miri tells them, shooing them away.

"We're too big," Nava says.

"You are until you aren't. It comes back around," Miri says, "and then you dream all day of napping again."

"And you also go back to diapers," Hayim says, "and also to no teeth." This cracks him and his sister up to no end.

Shuli frees his hand from Miri's and twists around to pat Hayim's cheek.

"This is true too," Shuli says. "But your parents want some privacy."

"Is it secret?" they both want to know.

"You want secrets?" Shuli asks, because he really has one these two might like. He'd bought a bag of candy for Gavriel and filled a second to give the children the next time they brought home good grades. "I hid a mountain of sugar under the sink," he says. "Now go rot your teeth."

They're gone in a flash, and Shuli, feeling the moment is anyway lost, stands up to follow. He looks to Miri, sad eyed. "What if I can't get my birthright back?"

"If God wants you to have it," she says, "you will."

·   ·   ·

SHULI FINDS THE KIDS ON THE LIVING-ROOM FLOOR AND talks them into forking over a stretch of candy buttons stuck to their paper strip. He sits cross-legged beside them, gnawing away, and thinking about what Miri said. Yes, if God wants you to have it, that's easy. But what if God doesn't? What if one is being tested and needs to show God the lengths to which he'll go?

Shuli ponders it all day, right up until they gather for Havdalah. It's Nava's turn to hold the braided candle, and Hayim is in charge of the *besamim,* passing the cloves under everyone's noses.

With the blessing done and the wine sipped, Shuli—on purpose this time—spills it into a saucer on the table. Shuli dips the wicks, putting the candle out, and as he does the smell of glim smoke mixes with the cloves and muddles with the taste of sweet wine.

He presses his fingers into the saucer and touches those wine-wet fingertips to his closed eyes, making his weekly wish. He opens them, blinking, the air still cool upon his eyelids, and already he's looking this way and that, shifty and nervous that Miri has read his mind.

They all wish one another a good week, and then Shuli slips out and goes straight into school. He returns on Sunday morning and Sunday night, facing an empty in-box each time. On Monday, he patrols the sidewalk in front of the yeshiva, waiting for Gavriel. He carries that nice big bag of kosher Paskesz candies, telling himself it's more than a bribe. It's a thank-you, and an incentive, and maybe a way to keep Gavriel from eating the *treif* ones on his own time.

As soon as he sees Gavriel, Shuli races over with the bag, pressing him to create another profile, another e-mail address, to help him lure someone at kaddish.com into writing back again.

"You want me to lie?" Gavriel asks, as he shoves a Sour Stick into his mouth.

"We already lied," Shuli says. "What's the difference now? Just eat your candy and make up someone dead."

And Gavriel does, creating losses, inventing tragedies, great and small, throughout the week. Shuli pops his head into Gavriel's other classes, pulling him from his studies without hesitation and plopping him down at a terminal in the computer room, sometimes kicking another student out of a chair mid-lesson.

The computer teacher, a woman who looks no older than Gavriel, appears to be having a panic herself. Reb Shuli has seniority, and Religious Studies has primacy, and Shuli knows there's something about the unbalanced confidence to how he barges in, unapologetic, that make the interruptions seem purposeful and beyond challenge.

As for Gavriel and Reb Shuli's endless stream of new profiles—which they kept track of in the spiral notebook that holds Eitan's original instructions—none of the related applications receives a single response.

"They know it's you," Gavriel says, matter-of-fact.

How they might know on the other end, Reb Shuli can't fathom. He asks Gavriel how they can possibly tell the real from the fake.

"We have their ISP address," Gavriel says. "I guess they've also got ours."

This leaves Shuli feeling so hopeless and unmoored, he fails at his attempt to whisper, yelling out, "How much longer will God punish me for one moldy crime?"

The computer teacher, along with her computer class, freezes. It seems they are waiting on an answer.

Shifting his gaze from terrified face to terrified face, Shuli wonders if he should share the answer. If he should tell them that his agony will end when he finds Chemi and makes a *kinyan* again.

But Shuli doesn't get the chance. The *rosh yeshiva*, Reb Davidoff, is already pushing through the door.

MRS. MEYERS CAN'T EVEN LOOK AT THEM, SO PREPOSTEROUS is the picture before her. In her decades of service to the school, she's clearly never seen a rabbi and a student in trouble together and sharing the bench outside the head rabbi's office.

Regarding the being-in-trouble part, Reb Shuli is impressed with Gavriel's calm—more composed, by far, than his teacher. And why shouldn't he be? The bench might as well have a little brass plaque with his name engraved on it, so often is he perched there, waiting to be sentenced.

It's over the nature of the offense that Shuli feels particularly bad. How confusing it must be for Gavriel, somehow in trouble for following a rabbi's orders, when he was always in trouble for exactly the opposite.

Shuli wishes he could take this occasion to tell the boy he'd done good, to shower him with more than candy for his valiant efforts, and to apologize for any difficulties suffered until now, and for the ones about to come.

Shuli would have liked to wrap up with a sincere prognosis for Gavriel's shining future, but on their hurried walk down the hallway, the *rosh yeshiva* had made clear that this little twosome was over and done with. That Reb Shuli wasn't to say a word in the moment and—after their stint on his punishment bench—to keep away from the boy, physically, verbally, electronically, and for good.

Steaming with anger, Davidoff had also mentioned a call he'd received from Gavriel's mother, spilling the beans. This made Shuli happy. Being ratted out in this way must mean that communication between mother and son was already improving.

When Mrs. Meyers answers her phone, she glowers at them both. Shuli takes a deep breath, combing at his beard with his fingers, waiting to see which of them has been called out of the batter's box.

Gavriel, reading the same signal, raises up his bottom and pulls his notebook from underneath. Rifling through, with an impressive amount of gravity, Gavriel finds what he's after and tears out a page. It zips free with a spiral-paper ripple that, even steeped in dread, Shuli appreciates as a lovely sound.

He passes the page to his teacher as Mrs. Meyers orders Gavriel to his feet.

Shuli, condemned to silence, says nothing and simply looks down.

On that piece of paper is a sweet, hand-drawn map of the area where the kaddish.com yeshiva is located. It's the drawing the boy had been working on in the computer room the previous week, and which Shuli had rejected as the poison fruit of the digitized world.

Shuli's heart races as he reads the names of the cross streets, written in stiff, Hebrew-student letters. He looks at the box in the center, meant to be the building, and marked in red pencil with a dramatic, treasure-map "X."

Oh, this special child. Reb Shuli is overcome.

"I thought you might want it. Even if you didn't want to see the picture on the screen," Gavriel says aloud, in his normal speaking voice. Shuli stares up at Mrs. Meyers in abject terror. This boy, he is a model of how to be. Living his life, bold and unafraid.

Gavriel takes the handle of the *rosh yeshiva*'s door.

"The information. It's out there, Rebbe. This part is not a sin."

part three

XVII

To look down from the sky upon a place is one thing. To walk the streets, to hunt in real time and real space, humbled by one's 1:1 human scale, is wholly another.

Here, in the dark, with everything he'd brought stuffed into a knapsack borrowed from his daughter, Reb Shuli stands under a streetlight in Jerusalem and fishes out from its front pocket the map Gavriel had drawn. He contrasts that stark sketch with the city around him, wondering what he'd done.

As always, Shuli turns to the Bible for comfort. How many of its stories were meant to aid a pilgrim in exactly his straits? How many tales intended to support the faithful through the weariness of just such a night? He takes stock of the wonders revealed to those rash in their faith and patient in their quests, the wayfarers rewarded for bad judgments made with good reason.

Shuli thinks he may be, right then, only feet from the yeshiva's front gate. What if he shares that very streetlight with Chemi, its halo sneaking through some window and brightening the pillow where rests that righteous man's head?

As tantalizingly close as he might be, Shuli folds his map and walks toward the center of town, to check into his overpriced, no-star hotel.

MIRI HAD SNIFFED OUT HIS PLAN BEFORE HE'D SAID A WORD. She'd come into the kitchen, her nose wrinkled, to find dinner already cooking, the dishes washed, and her husband home hours ahead of schedule. His jacket hung on the open stepladder and Shuli stood at the fleishig sink squeezing the suds from the sponge. He had his sleeves rolled, half for chores and half for the argument ahead.

"Whoever heard of a teacher being suspended, along with a student?" Miri said as soon as he'd told her. "It's absurd."

Gavriel had been given only a day—which would not go on his record. Shuli was put on ice for two weeks, the first, without pay, as sanction, the second, back on the rolls, for mental health.

"Those are the reasons Davidoff told you," Miri said. "It's all probably just to give that traumatized computer teacher a break." She'd then lifted the lid on a pot and tasted the soup Shuli was making.

"Are you sure you're not fired?" Miri asked, dipping her spoon again and blowing the steam his way.

"Not fired. Not yet. I'm pretty sure."

She'd relaxed her shoulders so precipitously that Shuli saw them drop. Her tone had also softened, as she asked what he planned to do.

"Make big dinners," he'd said. "Do more laundry. Cull the bookshelves—"

"I don't mean for your suspension. I mean what are you going to do about letting this craziness go?"

"Let it go? I can't. Not until I track down Chemi. He's obviously the one who told them not to answer."

"Who, the website? Why in God's name would he do that?"

"Maybe he's taken a vow, like a *Nazir,* pledging never to be thanked, never to be found, committed to doing his selfless work unsullied. It's the only thing that explains it. It is the only thing that makes any sense. For kaddish.com to avoid me in particular, for them to spurn me like this—it's basically proof that Chemi is involved. I need to get him word that all I want is the burden of my grief back and then I'll leave him alone."

And that's when he told her what he'd secretly wished for during Havdalah, explaining why he saw the time he'd been given as a sign from above.

Miri had listened with compassion and then shook her head.

"With such a scheme, you may end up getting your grief back in spades. You'll grieve for the credit cards maxed out to pay for the trip, and for the job lost when Davidoff finally grasps how bananas you truly are and fires you for real. You can mourn for the wife who eventually leaves you after she finishes yanking out, in frustration, every last hair tucked under her wig."

This last one had knocked the wind out of Shuli.

"You wouldn't leave me?" he'd asked her, honestly afraid.

Just remembering it gives Shuli a shiver in the tiny bed, in his tiny hotel room. In answer, Miri had taken her time before sharing a kind of warning. "I can tell you I'd never leave you. I can also tell you that what makes any marriage work is the knowledge that no relationship should be taken for granted. That there is always a line where the one who'd never leave you is suddenly gone."

"How can you say that?"

"Me?" Miri laughed. "Who wouldn't threaten leaving in response to a husband already planning to go?"

"It's a few days. At most a week. I'll be back before my suspension is done. You and I have dedicated our lives to saving Jewish souls. What about saving mine? The Book of Life," he'd said. "How many free passes have I already been given, that I still live from year to year?"

"After all the good you've done, you think for one youthful mistake God will call back your soul? You really believe that's how Heavenly justice works?"

"If I'd acted out of ignorance, then no," Shuli said. "But even then I knew better. Even then, I was already not so young."

The Book of Life, it was not a joke, not to him and not to Miri.

It was an actual record that one was very literally written into and—God forbid—out of, each year. Annual judgment was neither concept nor idea, it was a serious verdict, life-threateningly real.

And Shuli had known as he raised it that Miri wouldn't want to risk ignoring his plea.

She took up his jacket and, folding it, laid it on the counter. She then lifted the open stepladder and carried it into the living room. Shuli, unrolling his sleeves, followed behind.

She climbed up and pulled the ancient family Bible from the top shelf of a bookcase, loosing a rain of dust and flakes of old leather along with it. Stepping down, facing Shuli, she'd opened the back cover to reveal the family tree written inside and an envelope with the last of the Clinton Hill money, their emergency fund.

"For your journey," she'd said. "May it be enough to buy back what you gave away."

They counted it out together. It was $2,750, almost a dollar for each of the prayed-for souls listed on the kaddish.com site. Symbols, serendipities, they were everywhere Shuli looked.

"Are you sure?" he'd said.

Seeing his anguish, understanding—as he'd hoped—Miri addressed him with love.

"I'm sure," she'd said. "Just do your best. One can't be expected to do more. Now go call Eli Steinberg to find a cheap flight. And tell the kids what you're up to—that part's not on me."

Shuli leaned over and kissed her, and his wife kissed him back.

"Only remember," Miri told him, "if you don't find what you need over there, in this life it's permissible to forgive oneself too."

XVIII

O F ALL THE BEAUTIFUL NEIGHBORHOODS IN THE WORLD, IS
any as lovely as Nachlaot in the early light of day? There's
the Jerusalem stone, and the Spanish-tiled roofs, and the mazes
of side street and alleyway, on which even those used to the laby-
rinthine layout of the city find themselves lost.

Shuli had spent time in Nachlaot before. He'd hung out in the
area as a stoned and wanderlusted Larry, and when he'd returned
to Jerusalem for his rabbinical studies, he'd whiled away many a
relaxing *Shabbos* there during that stint.

He knew about the tricks the neighborhood played on a visitor's perceptions. There were mansions tucked behind rotted
metal gates, and hovels where one expected a mansion to loom.
A single-story cottage might actually be three stories tall as it
climbed down a hillside, and some cave-like house might offer,
from a rear balcony, a breathtaking view.

It's that simple, sleepy mystery that Shuli adored. He found
it a joy to be lost there, except maybe when trying to locate a
specific computer in that crazy jumble of a place. Shuli comforts

himself with his proximity. A house of study can't be that hard to find at the edge of a single junction.

Standing more or less where he'd been the night before, Shuli holds out his map. He doubles back a bit toward center city, aligning himself with the intersection of the two roads Gavriel had drawn, the boy's red "X" marking where the building lies.

Shuli walks up and down the busier of the two streets first. A row of connected houses runs along the thoroughfare, their modest entrances opening directly onto the sidewalk. There's no yeshiva to be seen on either side and, on that stretch, not even a storefront to be found.

At the corner where he began, Shuli turns onto the other street, following it toward the *shuk*. Nothing there remotely fits the bill. And with a dull ache starting up in his stomach and a goodly throb to his head, Shuli crosses over to explore the one remaining arm of the map's axis, entering the Bukharian ghetto, where the neighborhood ends. A few paces in, Shuli spies an archway set between buildings and takes the passage running through.

On its far side, in place of a courtyard, is a vertiginous flight of stone steps. Tottering down to a landing framed by two high walls, Shuli looks out over the crowded mix of new construction and tumbledown houses split by an alley that ran parallel to the main street he'd first checked. It was a messy little block, made messier by the web of wires and cables running from the buildings in every direction, as if, were Shuli's hands big enough, he could make the whole block dance like a marionette.

At the bottom of the staircase, a pair of trash cans already sour in the morning heat. Just beyond them is a woman in a bright headscarf, fully ignoring Shuli. She's busy with a collection of laundry racks propped in the middle of the alley. They aren't hung with laundry, but covered with parchment paper, atop which she sets out circles of eggplant, transferring them from a washtub resting on her hip.

One of the racks is already full-up with slices of eggplant, heavily salted and sweating out their bitterness in the sun. By the size of the operation, the woman either has two dozen kids or owns a restaurant nearby.

"Excuse me, ma'am," Shuli says, polite, in his Brooklyn-accented Hebrew.

Acknowledging him, the woman takes up the long tail of her headscarf and wipes at her face.

"What is it?" she answers in English, as every Israeli who hears his accent does.

"I'm looking for a yeshiva," Shuli tells her.

At that, she laughs and laughs.

"You want to find a yeshiva in Jerusalem?" she says. "Throw a stone. Pick a door. You can't go wrong here."

"Well, oddly, for me it's already not been so easy. I'm looking for a specific one. In this neighborhood."

"As I said," and she offers up the whole of the city with a glance.

The woman rests the plastic bin on an empty rack and again wipes her face, this time dabbing between her eyes at the faint dip of hair where her eyebrows meet.

Seeing that Shuli is less than satisfied with her answer, she says, "I wasn't kidding. Go check with the tax authority. Half

these places are registered as study halls, and the rest as syn-
agogues. There is a puddle behind the next house over that
receives a hundred thousand shekels a year. A stipend from
the city for a ritual bath you couldn't wash a foot in." She then
looks Shuli up and down. "You're not with the tax authority,
are you?"

"No," he says. "A tourist. I'm just looking for a yeshiva
that I know, for sure, is nearby. Either up there, or here on the
bottom."

"If you were sure, you wouldn't be asking directions."

"My mistake," Shuli says. "But I really think it could be on
this block."

The woman seems to take a shine to his contrition or his
politeness, or maybe his soft American way of being. She says,
"Why didn't you say 'on the block' at the start? If you want a
real yeshiva, we've got only one. It's by the other staircase," and
she points to the far end, where Shuli now sees a second staircase
mirroring the one he came down. "There's a house in front. Back
behind is a small hall where the young men learn."

IT'S AS THE WOMAN DESCRIBED. BEHIND A SHACK OF A
house stands a plain, one-room yeshiva that looks as if the neighborhood had gone up around it. He steadies himself against the
doorframe, unable to believe he might actually be here.

Inside are two rows of three tables, with students studying in
pairs all along. At the front, a Holy Ark rests curtained against
the eastern wall.

The students at the tables look Shuli's way when he enters.

The hum of study stops for an instant, and then, like the sound of crickets in the night, it all picks up again. There is one student standing in the far corner and busy nodding in conversation with a bear of a man who Shuli assumes is the *rosh yeshiva*. The man has his back to Shuli, and, clapping the boy on the shoulder, he heads out a side door.

Immediately, the standing boy approaches, a welcoming expression on his face. He, like all the others—like Reb Shuli himself—is wearing a white shirt and a black suit, a black hat upon his head. As grown-up as the uniform is, the beard on this boy has barely come in. Even worse than the gossamer beard are the *peos* hanging impossibly thin at the sides of his ears.

Back when Reb Shuli himself was a teenager in yeshiva, he'd cut his own *peos* a bit too short for his father's liking, an early hint of the rebellion to come. His father had pulled him into his study and said, "You know, when the Messiah will arrive to carry us all to Israel, he will reach down and pick the boys up by their *peos*, and the girls by their braids. With a haircut like that," he'd told Shuli, dead serious, "you will be left among the Gentiles in *galus* to share in their judgment."

Recalling this, Reb Shuli thinks it's lucky that the boy is already here. The thought puts a smile on Shuli's face, and the boy, seeing it, smiles back. He shakes Shuli's hand and asks how he can be of service, and Shuli is amazed at how much easier a *yeshivish* Hebrew is for him to understand. He answers in Hebrew, telling him that he's a visitor from America.

The man who'd gone out the side door now returns through the front. He is maybe Shuli's age, and—carrying his hat now—noticeably bald. What little hair is left surrounding his *kippah* has already turned white. A formidable, unhealthy-looking belly pushes out against his shirt.

He is indeed the *rosh yeshiva*, and he is as warm as the student who'd approached. He introduces himself as Rav Reuven Katz, and the student as Gilad. Shuli stutters, then stops, saying nothing. He's suddenly afraid that this is the man who's been ignoring his appeals. If kaddish.com is run from this place, Shuli might need a more nuanced approach before identifying himself and admitting that he's the one who'd been writing, now come around the world to get back what was his.

Reaching for another name, he almost says "Larry," and then proceeds to blank on every boy he's ever taught, aside from Gavriel—an option as bad as using his own. What he ends up spitting out is "Shaul," the formal version of Shuli, and he shakes both men's hands again firmly as he does so.

Reb Shuli knows he's already involved in another form of deception, a terrible way to begin. He feels a tinge of cowardice at his action, but he'd come so far, and it was all so delicate. So he says he's heard wonderful things about them. And, if it's all right, he's come to learn Torah for the day.

Rav Katz partners him with Gilad. As soon as they're seated across from each other with their Gemaras open, Reb Shuli sneaks out his worn and pockmarked picture of Chemi, sliding it from his pocket and into view below the table's edge. He isn't trying to match a face, as there's no one, except Katz, within a dozen years of what would be Chemi's age. It's the room in which he sits that he's hoping to link to the image.

Tilting his head, trying to approximate the angle from which the photo was shot, Reb Shuli can see in the ceiling's dome, and the window's shape, a definite echo. And, as if the photo was taken at that exact same time of day, a patch of sunshine drops down on one of the tables.

How close he must be to putting things right.

The boy, eager, dives into the day's learning, and Reb Shuli tucks the photo away. The pairing is a good one. The study goes smoothly, and he and Gilad soon find a delightful synchronicity in the way that they interpret the text, with the boy deferring to his obviously educated guest. Shuli, fully inspired, raises up a thumb and, as if conducting a symphony, waves it about as they progress.

It's everything, this moment. Such a chance Shuli had taken. And here he is on day one, and he'd already found the yeshiva, right where—God bless him—Gavriel said it would be. At this pace—who knows!—he might locate his Chemi by nightfall and get back home with some of the Clinton Hill money in his pocket. He'd return to his wife and his children, a complete and fulfilled man. He'd put his arms around Miri, thanking her for her support, and hand over their rainy-day envelope proudly. He'd stand back and watch her note that it remained thick with cash.

He'd not even miss a *Shabbos*. And it's that *Shabbos* that Shuli pictures from Jerusalem, as if looking down on his family from above. He includes himself in the tableau, a father at one end of the table, a mother across, and a son and daughter, each occupying their point on the compass. And his breath is taken away as he sees below him his own good fortune.

Back in the dining room, with Miri's eyes resting upon him, Reb Shuli would get up, stepping west, then stepping east, blessing both of his children, pressing his palms to their heads, again laying hands, and uttering the benedictions himself.

Reb Shuli sits with Gilad, learning for hours more. He eats when they eat, and davens with them when it's time for afternoon prayers. When one of the boys stands up to say Kaddish, Reb Shuli covers his eyes with a hand as if in concentration, hoping his tears might disappear into the fullness of his beard.

XIX

STARING OUT HIS HOTEL WINDOW, REB SHULI REMINDS himself to get presents for the children and something nice for Miri. It's past midnight, but Shuli is amped up and still on New York time. He grabs the remote control for the TV and wonders how many years it's been since he'd held one in his hand.

Shuli fights off the temptation and, unbuttoning his shirt, kicking off his shoes, strips down to his skivvies for what he imagines will be another sleepless night. Triumphant as day one at the yeshiva had been, he doesn't call Miri to boast, afraid he'll give himself the evil eye.

He curls up under a stiff hotel blanket. He recites the *Shema* and sings *HaMalach HaGoel,* as he has at the children's bedtimes every night since they were born. He hopes the words will travel, making the journey across the oceans and reaching Royal Hills before the kids conk out. Shuli closes his eyes and pictures the children. Despite himself, he drifts off and sleeps well.

And while sleeping, Shuli dreams.

· · ·

REB SHULI'S FATHER APPEARS TO HIM, AN OCCURRENCE that has become sadly rare. Shuli notes himself noting this in that other realm. He's also aware that, despite being together in the same kitchen-like room, his father is sort of still dead and sort of alive. They face each other across a counter, and when Shuli looks down he sees it's piled with food.

It's a lavish spread, fresh and fragrant, kosher to the highest standards, and somehow stretching on, so that there's space for every delicacy one might ever want. He and his father must have washed their hands and said the blessings already, because neither pauses before making the move to eat.

But when they reach out so that they might partake of a beautiful, braided challah—its crust an egg-wash gold, fat raisins poking through—they discover that their arms are locked and rigid. Their limbs rise up from their sides as stiff and straight as boards. Apparently God had, in His infinite wisdom, taken their elbows away.

Reb Shuli's father makes a sort of desperate *whoop-whoop* sound. It's the kind of noise that might emit from a man's mouth if he were both human and bird, all at once. How strange!

In the dream, Reb Shuli chooses to look past that strangeness, focusing instead on the urgency behind his father's call. He interprets it as a cry of hunger.

While pondering the challenge posed by their new arms, and looking at the feast set before them, Reb Shuli, who alone has the capacity to talk, says, "Yes, yes. Of course!"

He remembers this exact scenario from his father's teachings.

This—what they were experiencing—was like that infinite table from the World to Come. It was another iteration of his father's Heaven and Hell, conjoined and sharing space.

He knew the two options for how this particular eternity might unspool. If Shuli and his father ended up being both selfish *and* elbowless, they'd stand there for all time, staring and starving. They'd hold handfuls of food at arm's length, struggling and failing to feed themselves, while the delectable smells of that otherworldly banquet rose up. Their greediness would commit them to a mouthwatering Hell.

But if they felt kindly and generous, caring, a son for a father and a father for a son, they might—as Reb Shuli does—reach across with ease so the other might eat.

With his unbending, staff-like arms, Shuli takes up fork and knife, cutting bite after bite, and lovingly feeding his hungry, birdlike father. And, feeling nurtured, his father wields his own straightened arms to feed his selfless son.

Oh, how his father's lessons had paid off, Shuli thinks. And, oh, what a blessing for his father, who'd died before Reb Shuli had returned to the fold. What a gift it must be to see his son before him, bearded and head covered, the impression of the tefillin's straps still visible on Shuli's outstretched arm. Shuli can feel, as actual heat, the warmth his father exudes.

It leaves Shuli overcome with an enormous sense of ease. His father, likewise at peace, steps back, properly gorged, his stomach noticeably distended. Shuli stands on tiptoes and braces himself against the counter. He then leans forward, his own stomach grazing the food, so he can unbutton the top button of his father's pants, as his father had always done after a big meal.

Shuli watches as his father's chest rises, better able to breathe his un-breath. He wonders how long his father will stay full, and how long they both might be this deliriously happy, which reminds him that there's something he should probably tell his father if what they're sharing is to be as pure as it feels.

Shuli squints, wondering if his dead-but-somehow-not-dead father will gaze at him with such pride when he knows about the Kaddish. When he knows about the opportunity Shuli had squandered. When he understands he'd been abandoned the week after he was gone.

Shuli isn't sure if it's in reaction to the concern on his face, or if a new bout of hunger has struck, but his father makes that *whoop-whoop* sound. He does it in a loop turned monstrously shrill. With his pants already drooping, his father toddles to the edge of the counter, his mouth open like a baby bird's.

Shuli just wants to silence that noise. He knows he can't cover his ears, so he picks up the dream knife and the dream fork. He hurries to cut a bite, to feed his father, to shut that mouth. And Reb Shuli finds, to his terrible surprise, that he's lost control of his new arms.

They flail and strike about, knocking plates to the floor, tipping bowls of fruit, slicing at the air.

As is natural in such an instant, especially when unused to the fact that one's elbows are no longer, Reb Shuli steps instinctively forward, so that he might right some of the plates he's tipped over, so that he might scoop back some of the fine foods tumbling to the floor.

But with those arms rigid before him and out of control, he overshoots his mark, his dream turned nightmare. He watches himself looking on helplessly as his arms swing, stabbing at, and slicing up, his sweet, sweet father, whose eyes are now agoggle. Under attack, his father only appears more birdlike, his tongue darting, his squawk getting louder, and his shirt, as if feathered, in tatters. Beneath it, the blood beads along the jagged lines.

IN THE MORNING, REB SHULI WASHES HIS FACE AND HANDS, still shaken from the upset that was his fleeting taste of sleep. He bends his elbows, relishing in their mobility. He then wraps his tefillin and prays, haunted by the dream and the intrusive image of his father's frightened eyes, the gaping mouth, and that terrible spear of a tongue.

If he'd been at home and hadn't already forgotten it all upon waking, he'd have convinced himself it meant nothing, at most making a nervous joke to Miri about his trigger-happy subconscious. But Shuli knew very well where he was. And for the dreamer in God's Holy City, similar visions have held great significance before.

Dressed and sunscreened on what little wasn't bearded, Shuli heads right for Nachlaot. He passes the corner with the arch, walking on to the next, as yet unexplored. There he finds the second archway that leads to the far stairway, the one closer to the yeshiva's entrance.

When he reaches the alley, the woman with the headscarf waves to him from the other end. Shuli waves back. The woman waves again, more fiercely, drawing him her way.

She's once more busy at her laundry racks. Today, it's not parchment paper and eggplant, but baking trays of toasted sunflower seeds, their shells glistening as she spreads them out in a layer.

"Is that the place you were looking for?" she asks Shuli in English.

He tells her that it is.

"They are nice boys there. Very polite."

"Do they come to your restaurant?" Shuli feels rather smart as he says it—for she'd not said a word about what she does.

"It's a stand in the market. Not a restaurant. I only do takeaway."

"Does that mean the seeds are for sale?"

Shuli's stomach grumbles loud enough to hear. More than the breakfast he'd skipped, he was ravenous from his violent dream feast.

Fishing a folded twenty-shekel note from the inside pocket of his wallet, he gives it to her. She passes it back to him, laughing.

"What's funny?" Reb Shuli asks in Hebrew, somehow wounded.

His Hebrew makes her laugh even more, so that Reb Shuli sees all the fillings dotting her teeth. He repeats his question in English.

"I don't know where you got it from," she says. "But that kind of twenty hasn't been used in forever. It's not worth anything anymore."

"It's from my last trip to Jerusalem."

"And you kept that money in your wallet all this time? Like a teenager with a condom?"

Shuli blushes. And he knows she must think it's because of her racy talk. But it's the reason he keeps it that has him glowing red.

For he's again stung with the reminder of all he'd rejected that he now embraced. Back when he was living as Larry, he'd laughed louder than this woman when his father had begged him to at least prepare for the end of days. The old man was frightened Larry would be left behind. He'd told him of the tzaddikim among them, of Larry's neighbors in Brooklyn who quietly waited for the Messiah's return, Jews who literally kept their suitcases packed and ready, so that they might not waste a second in following the *Moshiach* home to Israel when he called.

To Shuli, who now waited for the ingathering himself, the suitcase seemed a step too far. But he admired the conviction behind it. And when he'd last left Israel, he'd kept that twenty as mad money for when the *Moshiach* brings the world's Jews back to the Holy Land. Shuli thought it might be nice to be able to buy a cold drink or a falafel when they arrived.

The woman with the seeds tells him to wait. She slips through the solid metal gate in the wall behind her, leaving it ajar. Shuli spies the sky-blueness of her front door through the space the open gate makes.

She returns with a wax paper bag and begins serving up an order for Shuli.

He puts his twenty-shekel bill back in its place and from his back pocket produces the envelope of dollars with which Miri had sent him off.

This time, without laughing, the woman tells him to put his money away.

"It's all right," she says, and hands him the seeds, still warm.

"I couldn't," Shuli says. "It's your *parnasah*. To take from a stranger. You must have your own family to feed."

"Such a pilgrim as you, with that sad, worthless bill stashed away. This I don't get outside my door every day."

XX

WHEN SHULI BUILDS UP ENOUGH COURAGE, HE FOL-
lows Rav Katz out the side door to the little patch of
dirt between the yeshiva and the perimeter wall, where the *rosh
yeshiva* goes to smoke.

Before Shuli has a chance to feel awkward, Katz shakes a
second cigarette loose, which Shuli accepts. Katz holds up his
lighter, giving it a flick.

Shuli leans into the flame.

"Thank you," he says, in Hebrew. "For the cigarette, and for
the hospitality. It's nice of you to make room."

"Why wouldn't we? It costs us nothing to have our learning
lifted higher by yours."

"Not everyone is so welcoming. Who hasn't walked into
a shul in some city and felt everyone looking him up and
down?"

"That's not been my experience," Katz says. "The opposite,
even. But I'm glad we're not that way. Especially when our visitor has so much to offer. I watched you yesterday. You must be
a rebbe yourself, in the States."

"I am," Reb Shuli says. "But that Gilad is naturally gifted. A very smart kid."

"This whole group is especially strong." Katz pauses to sniffle and then sneeze. He looks up, eyes watering. "Remind me again how you found us?"

"A friend. Actually, a friend through your website."

"Our website?" Katz says, now staring Shuli up and down— exactly in the way Shuli had just described.

Shuli first nods and then shakes his head, trying to read the correct response on Katz's face.

The rabbi helps him along. "A website, thank God, is something we don't have. And don't want."

"If it's bad to mention," Shuli says. "If it's private."

"A private website?" And now Katz looks more confused than suspect. "Better, let's switch to English, so instead of me not understanding you, you can have the pleasure of not understanding me." Katz shows Shuli his palms and wipes the slate clean. "Let's start again. You're saying it's the Internet that brings you by us?"

And what is Shuli to do but proceed?

He holds his cigarette out to the side, before taking a deep, smokeless breath. Shuli says, "There is a site. It's for Jews who need to say Kaddish for a loved one but don't want the responsibility. Through this service, they hire someone. They can employ a student to say the prayers."

And from Katz's expression, Shuli's not sure if the *rosh yeshiva* understands English at all. But then he sees it's the idea of it that Katz is stuck on.

"What kind of mamzer skips out on such a responsibility? What kind of dog would do that to the dead?"

"Well, it's not ideal," Shuli says. "But we can agree, the person who does that—at least he doesn't abandon. He does his duty! To find someone else, a *shaliach mitzvah*—which is perfectly kosher—it's so much better than the alternative."

"Is it?" Katz says. When Shuli doesn't answer, Katz points two fingers his way, the cigarette pinched in between. "Those who do nothing are truly ignorant. Or truly don't care. Or they are the ones whose hearts have been hardened by God, as He did with Paroh. It's very easy to see how their limitations might leave them without fault. But the person who'd arrange such a *meshugena* thing, it means that he knows how important it is, yes? It means he understands what he should do, and yet tries to wiggle out from underneath, as would a snake. To take such an action, it is worse than inaction. To me, the people who'd do it are even lower than those who'd leave a body unburied for wild animals to eat."

"You can't mean that," Shuli says, sweating profusely, so painful is the insult. However distressing it would be to hear this charge laid directly against him, it's ten times more hurtful when coming at him unadulterated and theoretical, a wise man's belief.

"Bottom line," Shuli says. "It's still better for the deceased's soul to have someone—anyone—saying the Kaddish."

Katz twists up his nose. He's not having it.

"Then why do we say 'Blessed is the True Judge' if the dead will not be treated fairly? The soul is judged based on the actions of a life."

"Let's not get into that. Forget the soul—"

"Forget the soul? What else is there?"

"In this instance," Shuli says. "I'm saying, for us to look more harshly—as judges, human judges—on one who takes steps to remedy, who tries in his own way to see that good is done . . . I'm simply asking, can't you see the beauty in that?"

Katz points to the house in front of the yeshiva.

"Pretend this house is on fire. Say I throw my cigarette down and the structure catches fire when we walk away. Pretend it's all wood, not plaster and stone. Pretend it burns easily, and—God forbid—there are people inside; those are the souls." He pauses to make sure Shuli is with him. "Now we put two bystanders outside. One does nothing, watching, useless, with his hands on top of his head, his eyes open wide—frozen that way. The other, knowing the gravity of what's taking place, knowing that someone must do something, approaches and spits once into the fire and then walks off. Which of them looks more beautiful to you? The one who does nothing, or the one who knows the size of the emergency and offers such miserly help?"

The cruelty of it—it's uncalled for. It's too much. "Miser?" Shuli says, nearly yelling. "To say 'miser' is unfair!"

"Misers! Why not?" Rav Katz says, unmoved. "It's a very good word."

Shuli, dizzy with hurt, remembers—yes—Rav Katz, if he's in charge of it all, in charge of the site, wouldn't he want to throw someone like Shuli off the scent? Couldn't this be on purpose?

Maybe others had shown up in the past wanting to undo a *kinyan,* or even to bring a gift and offer thanks. How many must want to meet the one who'd played such an extraordinary role in their lives? Yes, of course, why hadn't he thought this when he was sitting with sweet Gavriel in Brooklyn? How many such letters as Shuli's did Katz receive every day?

Katz smokes another cigarette in silence. Shuli can tell, with their heated talk, that the rabbi is taking Shuli's measure a second time. "Shaul," he says, "you really think we have such a site? That we take money for such a thing from the demons who'd pay?"

"Did I say that?" Shuli says. He can feel the door he'd opened closing on him.

"The website. You did say that. That we have one."

"No, no, I didn't. I was still speaking Hebrew. A misunderstanding. I was trying to tell you about a friend, a friend who builds websites—"

"You didn't say that. Not at all."

"A hundred percent, I meant to! I was trying to explain to you about a neighbor I said Kaddish with, when both of our fathers died—"

The true confusion on Katz's face has Shuli worried that he really may have arrived at the wrong yeshiva on the right block. The thoughts race and Shuli catches himself mumbling.

"Are you all right?" Katz says. "Everything OK in there?"

"Yes, yes." Shuli smiles a weak smile. "It must be the jet lag. It's like falling asleep on one's feet. Also, the cigarette. I haven't had one in a very long time. In America, they make it much more difficult to smoke."

"As well they should," Katz says. "It's a sin to poison one's body. I know that I myself must put up a better fight." He looks to the ground and grinds the butt he's already dropped into the dirt.

"About my friend," Shuli says, "the website friend. When he lived in Israel, he used to learn here, at your *beit midrash*. Maybe fifteen years back. Even twenty! Quite some time ago."

"You're in luck, then," Katz says. "Do you know how long I've been here? Since I was their age." He gestures to the students inside. "I grew up in this place. First I came to study, and then I returned to teach."

"Like me!" Shuli says, with an incredible amount of relief. It was a blessing to find a personal link. "I also am a rabbi in the yeshiva where once I was a boy. What are the chances?"

"This former student. Your friend," Katz says. "What's his name? If he's less than a thousand years old, I should know him myself."

Shuli doesn't see any other way to play it. He says "Chemi" aloud.

The rabbi keeps his cool, staring off as if running through his own mental census.

"A Chemi?" the rabbi says. "A Chemi that was a student here?"

"Yes, definitely. Definitely a student, and definitely here."

"We've had probably a hundred Yossi's and twice that many Moshe's. But over my whole tenure, a single Chemi, I can't recall." The rebbe seems to return for a moment to the list he'd conjured. "There was a French boy who came to us both for his *Shanah Aleph* and *Shanah Bet*. A *baal t'shuvah*. That one, he was a Remy, not a Chemi. Anyway, when he left after the second year, he was already for a long time going by Baruch. But I'm sure, it was Remy when he arrived."

"No, the name is as I say it," Shuli says. "I know it was Chemi—absolutely, for sure."

Shuli stands open and vulnerable under the rabbi's gaze. He presses his hands together before him. "Would you maybe try one more time?" Shuli asks, openly pleading. "Can you, as a kindness, think back?"

XXI

A CRUSHING WAVE OF FOOLISHNESS LEAVES SHULI UN-
steady on his feet. He very nearly says "What have I
done!" to Rav Katz before mumbling "jet lag" once more and
hustling out past the little house and through the front gate. He
hasn't been so undone since he'd run off from the wedding in
Royal Hills.

Shuli knows there's no other yeshiva camouflaged on that
alley or on the parallel street at the top of those stairs. He knows
it's not modesty that has Katz keeping kaddish.com hidden. The
facts are the facts. Shuli had found the yeshiva he'd been looking
for, but there was no team of students praying for hire, and no
minyan for mourners in some secret place. There was nothing
there to match what he'd flown around the world to find.

Still, Shuli believes—as much as he believes in anything—
that kaddish.com is nearby. And he trusts that his naughty
Gavriel, with his hand-drawn map, had put the "X" on the right
spot.

Thinking of the places right before our eyes that we cannot
see extinguishes in Shuli whatever hope he'd had. For wasn't

everyone in the world aware, right then, where the Garden of Eden waits? Wasn't it mapped out in the Bible as clear as can be, as clear as Gavriel's "X"? Couldn't Shuli right then make his way to the rivers flowing from it, the mighty Tigris and Euphrates, marked on Google Maps with the same names God gave them?

But if God doesn't intend for one of His servants to succeed— if kaddish.com was Shuli's very own Eden, an earthly ideal from which a flawed Shuli was rightfully expelled—it would, as with the other, remain a paradise concealed before him in plain sight.

He knows he should go back to his hotel, grab his passport and Nava's knapsack, and fly straight home. He could throw himself on Davidoff's mercy and be back in class that very day. Shuli could tell the whole truth, opening up about his failures, old and new. Who wouldn't feel compassion for him in his plight?

Shuli climbs the far stairs and follows the route up the hill, toward his hotel. When he reaches the top of the *midrachov* and spies all those happy people going about their business along the cobbled street, when the breeze brings the laughter of the high school kids, hanging out, and the lively sounds of the tourists discovering what's been discovered endless times before, Shuli thinks it might do him good to disappear himself, to be invisible for a little while in their midst.

Shuli hadn't given himself a moment away from his crusade. And the atmosphere cheers him instantly. Feeling hungry, he goes to the kosher Pizza Hut, its own kind of thrill. He sits outside and eats his pizza and drinks a gallon of Coke.

He watches everyone darting about with their plastic shopping bags, filled with hippy-dippy Tzfat candles, and DON'T WORRY AMERICA, ISRAEL'S GOT YOUR BACK T-shirts, and candy bars with Hebrew names. He sees a little *pisher* sprint by carrying a spiral shofar as tall as he is. Shuli remembers the presents for his family. If he was going home without the one thing he'd come for, at least he should bring gifts.

Shuli roams into a shop with a mountain of yarmulkes on display, all too small in diameter for anyone who truly fears God. He pokes around, picking up the *hamsas* and blue-glass talismans, and fiddles with the stone mezuzot and dreidels, the Armenian pottery, and the bottles of colored sand.

He's about to take another spin when he hears his name. Not "Shaul" but "Reb Shuli." And who is it—he'd literally just been thinking about the wedding—but Daphna Weider, the mother of the bride.

"I bump into your family everywhere," she says. "I saw Miri the day of the chuppah. And now, to see you here? *B'otot u'bmoftim,*" she says, with a wink. And, turning serious, "This can't be vacation with school on. Who's minding the store? The children must run wild."

"I came to learn for the week. A kind of sabbatical," Shuli says. It comes out as naturally as anything he's ever uttered. "And what about you?" Shuli asks, feeling light.

"The newlyweds are here. And me and Zev tagged along. We have an apartment in Rechavia that we don't get to near enough."

"Crashing your daughter's honeymoon, that's impressive— even for a Jewish mother."

"It's not as bad as it sounds, I promise. Tal is starting up at *kollel* and we came to check in for a month, maybe two, while they get settled."

"Well, remember to let the happy couple breathe."

"I promise they get plenty of time alone. And"—she winks

again—"I don't need you to mother me." Daphna goes off, buying nothing. Shuli watches her disappear into the crowd.

This is how it is for so many in their community, back and forth to Israel, as if it's nothing, as if one could take the Lincoln Tunnel and find Jerusalem on the other side. Shuli was much more likely to bump into someone from Royal Hills on Ben Yehuda Street than strolling around Madison Avenue at home.

Regardless, the odds of seeing her when he'd only just staggered away from the yeshiva, recalling her daughter's wedding of all things, is more fate than accident. He also knows that it's not the meeting but what she drew out of him that matters.

Shuli had lied to her. But the way it came out, the ease with which he'd said it, made Shuli reconsider. Did it have to be a lie at all? Wasn't he here on a sabbatical, to be used how he wanted? Hadn't Davidoff sent him off, and Miri supported the trip, and hadn't Shuli, from arriving in Israel, learned with vigor—with *kavanah*—from morning to night? And so . . . why not, yes, learn for one more day *l'shem Hashem*? He wasn't like the parents of his students, his well-off neighbors, with their apartments in Tel Aviv and Netanya, with their frequent-flier miles to spend. How often was he here? How clear was Daphna's message?

B'otot u'bmoftim, as she'd said. With signs and with wonders. It's as if she were an angel sent to find Shuli at his lowest, to help draw out the truth from inside his lie. Daphna Weider dispatched as God's emissary to help steady Shuli on his shaky feet.

Shuli pulls out his envelope of money. He fans the bills, calculating how much he must already owe the hotel, and how close he edged to putting the family in debt.

·   ·   ·

THE YESHIVA IS NEVER LOCKED. AND SHULI WAITS IN HIS seat at dawn the next day. He's brought his tallis and tefillin along with him, so that he might join the minyan at the study hall. It's a Thursday, a Torah reading day, and this he wants to hear.

When the others arrive, Shuli stands happily beside Gilad for *Shacharit*. Keeping Gilad in his thoughts, he prays for his study partner, such a wise young man. He prays for his family, for their good health and safety and comfort. He prays for Miri's continued support, and for her to, even a little bit, understand the choices he'd made.

While meditating on his beautiful children, he says a prayer for poor Gavriel. Let the boy be happy, let the boy feel loved. What he hopes, in an unformed, wordless way, is for the child not to end up like him—an existence half wasted on nothingness, and now spent trying to put that nothingness right. Shuli goes on to pray for the rest of the students flanking him. These myopic, zestful, tadpole scholars, among whom he relishes every second.

Shuli adds a prayer for his sister, Dina, in Memphis, and for his mother and her idiot husband in California, and for his father up above. He prays for the hardworking woman who prepares food in the alley, who Shuli pictures as forever wiping at her brow. And, of course, he prays for Chemi, wishing that he would, somehow, soon be found.

And, as happens, when the image of that pornographic woman flashes before his eyes, Shuli, guilty, prays too that she might be well.

The *parochet* in front of the ark is pulled aside, and the doors opened. The whole room stands at attention. Inside, the Torah is wrapped in its familiar red cover, silver bells crowning the finials and a silver breastplate hanging in its center.

One of the boys whispers in Shuli's ear, asking his father's name. Shuli would be called to the Torah to say one of the blessings. It's an honor offered to guests. But he likes to think they also acknowledge the fervency he'd brought to his learning and the new air of honesty he'd carried in with him that day.

At the last *aliyah,* they call Reb Shuli up.

He recites the blessings before and after the reading and then stands off to the side as the open scroll is held aloft for all to see. After it's rolled closed and its sash tied, the vestments are draped over the Torah's permanently raised, stiff, wooden arms—how much it was like his dream!

As its velvet coat is smoothed in place, and before the silver breastplate is again hung over the front, Reb Shuli sees the dedication embroidered into the fabric. The Torah had been donated by the family of David Yerachmiel Leibovitch.

At first he thinks nothing of it. Then he looks at that middle name.

What if this generous Leibovitch had wanted to mask his identity? What if, in service to a certain website, this person had not gone by his last name or first, not by Duvid or Duvele, Yerachmiel or Yuri, but instead used the second part of his second name? What if he'd long ago started signing his letters Chemi, staying connected to his true self, while putting a little distance between?

It's a stretch, Shuli admits. But how far a stretch was it when he believes, beyond the shadow of a doubt, that the kaddish.com computer is right there?

The more he considers it, the more it makes sense. It's a testament to the true power of faith! How many short minutes had elapsed since he'd prayed for Chemi to appear?

Shuli wonders if, even an hour before, the name on that Torah was the same as the one he'd just read. Maybe through yearning and supplication, the very letters had been picked up and rearranged by the holy hand of an outstretched arm. A shiver runs through him, just to think it.

XXII

SHULI IS USELESS AT LEARNING ALL MORNING, DELIRIOUS over his theory and the possible progress it portends. At lunchtime he invites Gilad to eat with him at one of the restaurants in Machane Yehuda—Shuli's treat.

Gilad leads the way, twisting and turning through the alleys with Shuli on his heels. As they cross Agripas, Shuli sidles up and asks if Gilad knows the woman who's always preparing food in the alley by the yeshiva, does he know which stall is hers, and if her cooking is kosher enough for them to eat.

Gilad does, and it is.

The woman greets Shuli amiably. "The seeds were good, then!" she says.

"They were," Shuli says. And, peering over at all she has on display, he and Gilad order *malawach* to go, rolled up and stuffed with *matbucha* and eggplant, and a number of fillings for which they didn't ask.

Shuli pays, and they eat while they roam. They drink ice-cold sodas and then stop off at Marzipan, the best bakery in the market. Shuli wants to buy a few kilo of rugelach to bring back for the others, a good sport.

As the pastries are boxed up, Shuli, trying for maximum nonchalance and desperate to grill Gilad, says, "The dedication on that Torah, I noticed it's from a *Mar* Leibovitch?"

"You know Dudu?"

"Dudu?" Shuli says, and already his confidence dwindles.

"He gets mad if you call him Mister or Rebbe. He's not a formal guy. He didn't even want his name sewn onto the cover. We bought it ourselves. Everyone chipped in—Rav Katz too. A person should be thanked for giving something so big."

"I couldn't agree more," Shuli says. "And does Dudu give you other stuff too?"

"He's our main donor. After what we get from the government, Dudu pays for pretty much everything else. Rav Katz always says that without him we'd be studying in the dark."

"These days, even to be an ascetic is expensive."

"And it's not just the big stuff, the Torah and new books when we need. He also does like you when he visits."

"Like me?"

"He brings sweets. And always caters a big meal. Then he learns with us, and tells us how proud he is."

"And he really doesn't ask for anything in return? Not for you to maybe say a *meshabeirach* for a sick cousin, or to dedicate your studies to someone's memory, maybe to say certain prayers?"

"What prayers would we say?" Gilad says.

"Like the Kaddish. Does he ask you, ever, to say the Kaddish?"

"But no one's dead."

"Of course," Shuli says, his heart sinking. "I just thought, even selfless, that he might ask that something get said."

"Nope. He always makes clear that he doesn't want anything in return. Except for the pictures for his wife and kids, he doesn't intrude at all."

The pictures! That's how quickly things turn. Shuli thinks he might weep.

"He photographs you?"

"While we study. They're not for him, though. He just likes to show his family what their money provides."

"What a do-gooder! What an altruist!" Shuli says, thanking the heavens, thinking *Baruch Hashem* and joy of joys. He grabs the boxes of rugelach and practically skips back to the yeshiva, going over this puzzle with great pleasure. A man who comes to take photos for his family in exchange for some cash stuffed in the *tzedakah* box might also be a man gathering fresh images for a website that advertises his numinous wares.

Still, this doesn't solve for Shuli the bigger mystery. Where are the students who actually say the Kaddish? Where was the prayer mill where the boys commemorate their allocated dead?

As they climb down the stairs to the yeshiva, Shuli asks when this Mr. Leibovitch comes to visit.

"Sometimes once a month. Sometimes every other. It varies."

"Once every other month?" Shuli feels sick.

Gilad, always trying to please, reads Shuli's obvious despair.

"Sometimes it's more frequent. It can be twice in the same month, even more."

Shuli makes a face.

"It's true!" Gilad says. "The visits come in waves. At least that's how it's been since I've been studying here."

"When was the last time you saw him?"

"I don't keep track. Two weeks. Three, or four. I couldn't say."

IT'S AFTER MIDNIGHT WHEN SHULI CALLS HOME TRYING to catch his family all together. The kids sound happy. Nava wants to know if he's still using her backpack, and Hayim wants to know if he's on the plane already, and his sister, in a sisterly way, tells him he's dumb for thinking their father is calling from the air.

Then Miri takes the phone. And Miri listens to the update. And what does Shuli expect she'll say to the news that he's staying on for a week, or two weeks, or two months to wait for Leibovitch to turn up?

Shuli reminds her that the dome could be the same dome from the picture he carries, and that the patch of light that falls on the table could be the same light. He tells her that computers run on math and don't make mistakes, and it's from this kind of exactitude that Gavriel's map was drawn.

Miri says, "You're supposed to teach on Monday."

"What sense would that make?" he says. "No one should be teaching children when they're broken inside. What good would it do to come back like this?"

"Are these real questions, Shuli? The good it would do is you not getting fired. And your children having a father at home, and your wife having a husband in bed."

"All of those only make sense if I come home full and not

empty. What use is a husk of a husband if there's nothing inside?"

"You want sense? Tell me, do they charge the same rates at that hotel for empty people and full? Who's going to pay for all this?"

"I'll figure that part out too. I won't bankrupt us. And I won't let my family down."

"You don't get to decide that, Shuli. We do."

And he knows, on that point, Miri's right.

"You do understand what this means to me," he says, "to finish my *t'shuvah,* to finally mend what I've torn?"

"And you understand I'm entitled to be furious, while also still supporting my husband."

"I do," Shuli says.

"Then remember what I told you before you left. If you fail, then you fail. Still, in this life——"

And Shuli, always a good student, finishes it for her: "It's permissible to forgive oneself too."

IF HE NEEDS TO STRETCH HIS CASH FOR WHO KNOWS HOW much longer, the hotel is something Shuli can't afford. He packs up after he gets off the phone and considers his options for the coming *Shabbat.* He could go to the Kotel to beg someone to take him in. He could track down the Weiders, or open up to Rav Katz or Gilad and stay with one of them. But among God's devoted, in God's chosen city, it was too painful to acknowledge the dereliction that had landed him here. This, Shuli couldn't bear.

At dawn he heads down, his knapsack stretched to the seams,

and checks out. He keeps the bag between his feet as he counts out the bills. To his other sins, Shuli adds theft. Not knowing how long he might be sleeping rough, he'd taken the towels from the bathroom along with the soaps.

He told himself he'd return the towels before he flew home. He planned on full restitution when he either found Chemi or conceded defeat.

While he waits for Rav Katz and the others to show up at the yeshiva, Shuli studies the statutes relating to ownership and property.

He then learns Gemara with Gilad all morning. When they finish what they need to get done for the week, the boy wishes him a good *Shabbos* and goes off. Shuli immediately returns to the laws around larceny, exploring the severity of his misdeed.

He keeps his nose to the grindstone as the last of the students peel off, until it's just him and Rav Katz, who now smokes inside the study hall.

The rabbi practically stands over Shuli, who pretends not to notice. With a cigarette hanging from his lips, Katz runs his fingers through his beard, separating it into two parts, twisting the ends—and hovering. Finally, Shuli gives up and says, "Do you want me to braid it for you, Rebbe?"

"That would be nice. I could use a new look."

Shuli now engages, raising an eyebrow and giving Katz his full attention.

"You have where to go for *Shabbat*?" is what Rav Katz wants to know.

"That's what this is about?" Shuli says. "I'm fine. A lovely hotel. I was going to stay here until the last minute, and then run and shop. There's just so much to get through." And Shuli gestures toward the books spread out on his table.

"Well, the *shuk* will close in not too long. The *Shabbat* siren sneaks up on you if you don't pay attention."

"Can I go shop and then come back after? I really do want to finish what I'm working on."

"Come and go as you please," Rav Katz says. "I hope I've made clear that you're always welcome." Then, staring with obviousness at Shuli's fat knapsack, he adds, "You're not staying with friends?"

"A lovely hotel," Shuli says, standing up. "But I'll take your advice and go get my *challot* now."

Reb Shuli heads to the market and buys sweet *challot* and a bag of rolls. He buys candles and a bottle of wine. He buys hummus and a huge bag of cucumbers. A feast!

He then stays at his table until that *Shabbat* siren goes off, catching him by surprise, as Katz threatened it would. Shuli lights candles right there using two glass teacups to hold them. He says his prayers and makes the blessings over the wine, aching for home all the while. Shuli says *Motzi* and eats a whole loaf of bread for dinner. Then, for no good reason, he dips into his stash of cucumbers, sitting there until the candles burn down, afraid of an accident on his watch.

Shuli then takes his knapsack and heads out to the alley and up the close stairs. At the top, he glides out into the middle of the road, walking the emptiness of what was a usually busy street. Shuli follows it down the hill into the park that borders the neighborhood.

He finds a bench set back, away from the street, and takes out a towel to use as a blanket. Reb Shuli lies down, with the bag under his head for a pillow, better off than Jacob and his stones.

Oh, how used to staring up at ceilings Shuli had become. Here, camping out in the lovely chill of a Jerusalem night, Shuli looks up and muses his nocturnal musings with nothing to impede them. Without a roof above, his gaze bears on and on into a star-backed sky.

XXIII

S HULI DOESN'T MISS THE IRONY AS THE DAYS TICK BY. HAD he sat with such dedication at his sister's house way back when, had he devoted himself to his father's shivah with the intensity with which he kept vigil for Chemi, he wouldn't be in the bind he's in now.

How hard Shuli works to stay there, at what cost to his family? He sleeps in the park. He washes himself in the bathroom the yeshiva boys use, which is attached to the little house out front. He eats lunch with the boys and dispenses with the other meals of the day. It is, for Shuli, a trial.

When sleeping rough begins to wear, Shuli moves to the floor of the study hall, figuring he's not only been welcomed but is now embraced. If they so happily share their days, how much of a sin could it be for him to use the space at night?

He borrows Gilad's cell phone to make quick calls to Miri, spending most of the conversation telling her that he's sure Chemi will surface anytime. Miri's support doesn't wane so much as morph into increased concern for his mental health. She worries over Shuli and over their collective familial well-being. His daughter is a different story. Nava gives him the cold shoulder when he asks to talk, at most bidding Miri to say hello on her behalf. Hayim is the only one who sounds happy to hear from him. He tells his father stories about his adventures, never once asking how Shuli is. Shuli listens with tears in his eyes and, looking at his watch, inevitably cuts the boy off, for Gilad won't take any money in return.

Another *Shabbat* passes this way, with Reb Shuli making sure that nothing about his behavior seems amiss. Aside from shifting his belt to the next notch in, he presents as upstanding as ever.

He answers cheerfully whenever Rav Katz asks about his accommodations or how his family is doing in New York. *"Baruch Hashem,"* Shuli says, or "Technology today, it's like having them next door."

Thinking himself successful in both attitude and demeanor, Shuli is surprised when Rav Katz arrives extra early one morning lugging a worn army duffel. He drops it on the table and steps out the side door.

From the placement of the bag in an otherwise empty room, Shuli takes it to mean he's meant to peek inside.

Unzipping it, Shuli actually gasps from the size of the bounty. Inside are fresh white shirts, and fresh white socks, and clean underwear. For cooler nights there is a sweater. There's a pillow and blanket. A tube of toothpaste. A bar of soap.

Shuli repacks everything and moves the duffel to the floor at his feet.

HOW THANKFUL SHULI IS FOR A CHANGE OF CLOTHES. AT sunup, he feels so much better pulling on fresh socks and, he's embarrassed to think it, the clean underwear that Rav Katz himself must have previously worn.

He even sleeps well, cozy in the sweater, his new pillow a *mechayah*.

Buttoning up a stiff laundered shirt, he does his best to tuck all the excess around back. Katz's clothes hang blousy on his frame.

Once he puts on his jacket, Shuli feels like a million bucks. A little rest, a little renewal, and his spirits are at their most formidable. Shuli is feeling as grateful for Rav Katz as can be.

Shuli has a productive day of study. He hardly looks up until evening, when all heads turn toward the open front door. The stranger who steps through it is beardless and dressed in jeans and a polo shirt. But his tzitzit hang out, and he wears a black velvet yarmulke of a respectable size.

"This could be him," Shuli thinks. What a perfect time to have his full faculties restored and to make a passably tidy impression.

The man sets his feet solidly to the ground. "The longer it takes me," he says, "the longer until you eat." At that, a pair of students hop up from their chairs and follow him outside.

"Is that Mr. Leibovitch?" Shuli whispers to Gilad, truly shocked by how young and modern looking he comes across.

"Him?" Gilad laughs. "He works at one of the *steakiyot* in the *shuk*. But when that guy shows up, it means Dudu's not far behind."

The books are closed, and the surfaces cleared, and onto the tables, a giant spread is set. The polo-shirt man scans the students and, choosing himself, volunteers a third helper to oversee the dinner.

One table is for the meats and another holds a beautiful array of salads, and stacked on yet another table is a pyramid of bread.

There is a table of sweets and sodas, and bottles of beer, which the boys throw back as if dying of thirst.

Watching these lovely young men in a state of joy, feasting on food after feasting on Torah, actualizes for Shuli an ideal version of his father's deathbed counsel and his disturbing stiff-armed dream. This, right here, might be what Heaven on Earth looks like. To see them in their abandon, Reb Shuli can think of nothing more pure.

Shuli looks to Rav Katz. Yes, time was being taken from Torah learning, the evening studies fully disrupted, but, much like awarding a triple recess, Shuli feels the rebbe has erred on the side of merriment for the greater good.

It's then that a little man, his face hidden beneath the broad brim of his hat, pops through the door.

KATZ CROSSES STRAIGHT TOWARD HIM, HIS HAND OUT-stretched. The boys fall in behind their rebbe, making a big deal over their guest's arrival. Some of the more confident, and drunker, even clap him on the back.

The visitor wears a plain black suit, and plain black shoes, neither more polished nor more scuffed than anyone else's in that dusty city. He's narrow in build but has a solidity to him, the kind of person that might surprise a larger man were they to fight.

This observation is followed, in Shuli's racing mind, by another hundred, all of which lead to the same place: This man has to be Leibovitch. And Leibovitch, very well, might be the one.

Katz silences them all and turns the floor over to the man, who wants to say a few words. He first asks for a beer for a *l'chayim* and then, raising it up, says, *"Im ein kemach, ein Torah."* One can't study on an empty stomach, which makes the room roar. And Shuli, loosed from his trance, recognizes how hungry he is.

Gilad, as if reading Shuli's mind, comes over with a heaping plate for his American friend. He presents it grinning, kind soul.

While Shuli shovels the food down, Gilad twists one of his gossamer *peot.*

"That's Dudu," he says to Shuli. "I told you he'd come."

"Chemi," Shuli says, his heart swelling. "My old pal Chemi has arrived."

part four

XXIV

DUDU REFUSES TO LEAD GRACE AT THE END OF THE MEAL. He won't hear of it, and calls for a *Kohen* to have the honor. The students chant *birkat hamaẓon* and then pair up again for a bit of extra study. While they learn, Shuli keeps stealing glances at Leibovitch, who chats with Katz on the opposite side of the room. So often does Shuli do it, an exasperated Gilad keeps hitting his hand against the table to draw Shuli's attention back to the text. It goes on like that, until Leibovitch pulls out his iPhone, at which point a giddy Shuli closes his Gemara outright.

Leibovitch works the room, smiling and laughing and pinching cheeks. Shuli watches transfixed as he begins taking pictures of the students. There are portraits and candids. There are selfies with Dudu—everyone making silly faces as they horse around. And interspersed are the occasional posed shots, Dudu giving direction. "You two, lean back," he says. "And you, make it serious, focus on the *sugya* like it's really giving you trouble."

When the students head home for the night, Leibovitch lingers, talking to Rav Katz. Shuli reads at his table, waiting for his chance—he just needs a second alone. When Leibovitch says good night to the rabbi and steps out the door, Shuli pushes back his chair.

He's at the door himself when Katz says, "Nice dinner, no?"

Shuli, holding the handle, answers, "Nice dinner, yes."

"A good man."

"Generous," Shuli says. Then, opening the door, crossing the threshold, he says, "Fresh air," tipping his hat and rushing toward the front gate.

Shuli steps into the alley and it's already empty. The panic. Shuli's heart. Could it have been more than a moment? How could Leibovitch be gone?

There's no movement in the deep shadows that puddle along the walls. No one climbs either staircase. No footsteps echo back. Listening hard, Shuli hears what he always hears at that hour, distant engines, and the scream and howl of stray cats.

Catching something in the corner of his eye, Shuli spins around to see a shirt swish on its laundry line. He can't imagine where Leibovitch has gone.

The only possibility Shuli can think of is if he raced up the close staircase at top speed, taking the steps two at a time. So Shuli does the same, his shoes barely grabbing on the slickness of the stone.

At the top, practically throwing himself through the arch, Shuli stands on an empty sidewalk, scanning a deserted street. No one turns the corner, scuttling up toward city center. No one sprints down to the park, where Shuli had slept.

Running back to the stairs, Shuli sidesteps his way down to the landing, which, like its twin on the other side, offers a commanding view of the block.

He looks back up the stairs. He looks down at the alley. Leibo-

vitch couldn't possibly have—as Shuli fears—vanished in place.
It's then he considers the rusted metal door set into the landing's
wall, at his side. Like countless others in the neighborhood, cov-
ering nooks where people keep their junk tucked away, Shuli
hadn't ever paid it any mind.

It was dented all over, it's lock jutting out, the cylinder askew.
Where a handle would go beneath, there was only a teardrop-
shaped hole torn in the metal. The only embellishment on the
door was a Star of David affixed near the top, welded in place.

When Shuli looks back to the lock from the Star of David,
he'd swear there'd been a change. As if a light that was on had
gone off. Or maybe he hadn't noticed how black that teardrop
hole had been before? What if there was more than a cubbyhole
behind?

Shuli gets down on his knees to peer through. Seeing nothing but darkness, he stands and dusts off the legs of his pants
and—what other options remain?—he begins knocking on that
door. He starts lightly, with an open hand, tapping as Gilad had
against the table. The more he hits, the more he's sure that, for
Leibovitch to pull off his disappearing act, this is the only door
that fit the trick. Shuli hits harder. He hammers urgently and
madly, using both fists.

He is going to bang until that door opens, or until Leibovitch
steps out of a shadow and makes himself known. He will pound
and pound until he finds relief, or until the ground splits from
the noise, rupturing and swallowing him up—putting an end to
his troubles.

Shuli does not let up until he feels, mixed into the rhythm
of his banging, a latch unlatch, and the metal door opens out.
Leibovitch pulls Shuli inside by his sleeve, jerking the door shut.

He flips the switch to what must be the light Shuli had registered, and Shuli finds himself on a balcony, built atop the roof of the house below. At its back is a little shed of a structure, almost a lean-to. Above them, another balcony literally hangs over, sandwiching this hideaway on a kind of mezzanine carved out between the alley and the street above.

"The boys could have followed you!" Leibovitch says. "If you wanted money, you should have asked me then."

Leibovitch reaches into his jacket and pulls out his wallet. And Shuli understands what he must look like in his rumpled suit and Katz's hand-me-down shirt, and how he must seem like, stalking this man and banging like a crazy person against his door.

Dudu takes out a fifty-shekel bill and hands it to Shuli.

Taking it, Shuli lines up the Hebrew in his head and says, "It's not money I need."

"Well, when you figure out what you're after, I hope your desire is quickly met." Dudu undoes the latch. "If you don't mind," he says, "my privacy—it's hard won. The students don't know I keep a room for when I visit. No one else has ever chased after."

Leibovitch inches the door open, peeking down the stairs and, opening it farther, looking up toward the high street. The coast clear, he tries to usher Shuli back onto the landing. But Shuli steps forward, hooking a finger through the teardrop hole in the door and yanking it closed with some force.

He slides the bolt.

"The pictures," Shuli says.

"What pictures?" Leibovitch wants to know.

"At the yeshiva. Tonight. The students say you take them for your wife."

"And the students told me," Dudu says, switching to English, "that you are an American who comes to study from out of nowhere with young boys."

"What are you saying?" Shuli says, appalled, and switching to English too.

"I'm saying, are you making trouble for me, or am I going to make trouble for you?"

The harshness of it. The lengths this man will go to protect.

Shuli moves to the front edge of the balcony. He takes hold of the iron railing meant to keep one from tumbling down to the house's garden below, and he stares out into the distance, once again startled by the miraculousness of Nachlaot. A few feet from the staircase, and the view between buildings, and over the rooftops, somehow reaches out into the valley, the lights of distant neighborhoods sparkling in the distance.

"Those pictures are not for your wife, now are they?" Shuli says, not only undeterred but feeling a rush of love for this man and his unerring defense of kaddish.com.

"She likes to see, to keep current. My wife takes such pleasure in supporting Rav Katz and his students, as do I."

"No," Shuli says. "They're for the website." He steps toward a window and tries to peer into Dudu's apartment. All he sees is his squinting reflection in the glass. "It's from here that you do it, yes? It's from here that it runs."

When Shuli turns back, Leibovitch stands there, unguarded.

"Who are you?" he says.

"Me? How can you not know? The efforts I've made to find

you." He shakes his head. "Around the world," Shuli says, "when you refused to answer."

Shuli walks up to Dudu and—the moment he's been waiting for—considers taking his hands.

"At first I wasn't sure," Shuli says, "but then I thought about it, Reb David *Yerachmiel* Leibovitch." And he runs through it all again. "I thought, a David can go by 'Dudu,' just as a Yerachmiel can turn into a 'Yuri.' But also he can be called 'Chemi' for short, if he were to go by the second diminutive of his second name."

"It's you!" Leibovitch says, astonished. "The madman from Brooklyn who doesn't give up."

It's rapture for Shuli. Hearing this is pure bliss. The madman from Brooklyn, exactly.

Shuli isn't sure if he should hug him, or bow down, or launch into one of the infinite speeches he'd prepared for this occasion. He settles on the simple and straightforward, the singular reason he was there.

"I've come to get back what's mine."

Chemi suddenly appears quite unwell. He goes to the rear wall and sits on an overturned pail.

"It's gone," Chemi says, before Shuli can even propose a reversal of the *kinyan*. "Every penny. You've come for the money, but the money is gone."

He shows Shuli his empty palms, to prove it.

"The money?" Shuli says, trying to make sense of such a thing, utterly baffled.

"A family to support, you must understand."

But he doesn't understand, not at all. He was there for his

rights. To make a deal in the other direction, so that he could again bear the burden of mourning.

"I've been expecting you," Chemi says. "You, or someone like you. The police, or a gang of thugs from the rabbinate to set me straight where I'm bent."

"Why bent?" Shuli says, honestly trying to make sense of what this man, his Chemi, was trying to tell him.

"If there's no money, do you want to hit me? It's the least I can do."

"To hit you? But why?" he says.

Shuli goes back to the edge of the balcony and looks down to the dome of the yeshiva, almost close enough to touch.

He gathers up all the terrible truths that, for some stretch now, he'd unconsciously been collecting. The nightmarish bits of thread he'd been storing away, like a magpie, to suddenly weave together.

Shuli walks to the window. He presses his face to the glass, framing his eyes with his hands, so that he may better see into the darkness. What he makes out, in that simple, sad room, are— flashing like fireflies—all those busy little router lights.

Shuli is back, standing before Chemi, not wanting to believe what he already knows.

"Where are the students?" he says. "Where is the minyan? I'm begging you. Take me to those who are hired to mourn."

XXV

THEY SIT FACING EACH OTHER AT THE TINY TABLE, IN the tiny apartment, surrounded by giant stacks of loose papers, and binders in knee-high mounds. There's a laptop on the floor, and a printer, and assorted backup drives of varying sizes. There's a cot against one wall, with file boxes forming a hedge in front. Along the wall opposite is a counter with a sink and a microwave, and a mini-fridge tucked below. The bathroom—a toilet and shower sharing a single tiled stall—is visible through the only interior door. And then there is the crate at their feet, cords snaking out, and the router, whose lights Shuli had seen blinking in the dark, broadcasting its terrible lies.

Chemi sips at a mug of tea and laughs a gloomy laugh.

"For that, you fly around the world after twenty years? Over some old dot matrix *kinyan* for an online Kaddish?"

"For my father in Heaven—for his soul and mine."

"What does it have to do with souls? A *kinyan* like that is bells and whistles, less binding than a handshake. That's really why you beat down my door?"

"The transaction stands," Shuli says, grabbing the table. "I gave you my birthright. I need it back. It's not yours to keep."

Chemi mulls this over. And the calm with which he listens drives Shuli mad.

"I left my kids for this!" Shuli yells. "My wife! My fucking job!"

Chemi sighs. He fishes in his jacket pockets and, standing, gives a twirl around, surveying the apartment. He then steps between boxes to the cot. Reaching over to the wall, Chemi lifts a little tin amulet from its nail.

"Here," he says. "A new *kinyan*. Give me back that fifty and I'll give you this." Shuli accepts it and passes back the fifty-shekel note Chemi had forced on him outside. "I hereby return what you came for. Mourning again belongs to you." And with that sour victory, Shuli closes his hand around the amulet, acquiring.

THEY SIT THERE GOING OVER THE AWFULNESS OF WHAT Shuli has uncovered. Whenever he feels like he comprehends the gravity of it, Shuli again takes in the extraordinary mess of folders and dusty binders, the massive sheaves of intimacies betrayed and trusts squandered, of souls left to burn.

Shuli has trouble holding on to the size of it and keeps circling back to the start. "In my case," he says, "on behalf of my dear, deceased father?"

"Not a prayer," Chemi says. "Not one."

"And the twenty-eight hundred? The people listed on the site?"

"Two thousand seven hundred and ninety-four," Chemi corrects him.

"They're real?"

"For each, a premium paid, and then—"

"A Kaddish unsaid."

Shuli squeezes his eyes shut and tries to multiply his personal pain, to expand it out to all those touched by this treachery. He blinks and stares at Chemi. "It's just—so many people."

"I'm as surprised as you by the number, but they keep coming. Sometimes once a day. Sometimes once a week. Let's say, every month, a dozen on average sign up to pay."

"But when I went back online to find you, the number went up twice right then."

"The big number, on the home page—that's real. But when you first log on, it rolls back a couple of digits before counting ahead."

"It knows to do that? You can program such a thing?"

"It encourages. The mourner feels like he's watching deals being done. It makes a customer less lonely when opting for a lonely choice. I do feel for them."

"You don't feel anything for any of us," Shuli says, at a boil.

"You think you and I are so different? So maybe I don't go by the letter of the agreement, but I see that the memories of these people are not erased." Chemi gestures toward his archive. "It's all here. Every contract. Every file. It's its own kind of memorial. I'm kind of like a son who knows what must be done but pays someone else to do it."

"Don't compare," Shuli says. "What you do, it's criminal!"

"So call the police."

But Shuli doesn't. Instead, he rubs his cheeks with both hands. He scratches at them, and then scratches furiously at his chin.

Chemi watches this agitated display. "Can I ask you something?"

Shuli stops and meets Chemi's eyes.

"How did you find me? All these years, I wait for someone to grab me in the street and tear me limb from limb. I wait for one of the students downstairs to figure it out and kick in my teeth. Yet, it's you. From way back at the beginning."

"I had a map. From a boy in my class, at the school where I teach. The boy who wrote you about his father."

"Still, it's impossible. There's no trail to follow from there to here."

"When you replied, we replied with a picture. When you answered, the boy looked inside the server for the IP address that attaches," Shuli says, repeating what Gavriel had taught him. "And with the latitude and the longitude, he found the satellite image of the street. I felt too guilty to look, an invasion," Shuli says, blushing. "So he drew a map of where you were. Unfortunately, not an exact map. Just the crossroads. But I thought it would be much simpler to find you when I thought kaddish.com was real."

"Very smart, and very sly. An x/y-axis. Truly, well done."

"When there was a yeshiva, but no you, and no computer, I waited. It's taken some time."

"Well, you couldn't have gotten any closer than you did. Jerusalem is a stacked city. It's not just the x/y. You need the z to give you the third dimension. It's admirable, though. What your hacker student accomplished, you can't have expected more."

"He is all of twelve years old. Smart child."

They both afford Gavriel a moment of esteem. Then Shuli takes the questioning back, feeling he's already shared more than Chemi had a right to know.

"And the money? All those clients," Shuli says. "You should be rich by now. How can it all be spent?"

"Do you have any idea what it costs to live here? Do you know what it costs to raise a family? This business, it's only by credit card. The transactions get reported. Do you know what murder taxes are in Israel?" Chemi says, in a huff. "It's almost better not to work. If you knew the hours I spend keeping the whole thing going. This scam is scamming me. And then there's the money I give to that yeshiva eating away—"

"Wait, wait," Shuli says. "Why give money? Why do anything for those boys?"

"Because it's their real faces in those pictures. Do you see how they live down there? On what little they survive? Don't I owe them for what they do?"

"You worry over the students but not the dead?"

"The dead are dead."

"And what of the living who pay?"

"The boys are different. They're innocent."

"And we're guilty?"

"Everyone who comes to my site gets what they deserve."

As quick as Shuli is to acknowledge his own guilt and the spectacular lapse behind it, he's not sure that's what anyone deserves, least of all not knowing they'd been treated in bad faith.

It's clear to him what must be done.

"The families need to be told."

"Great idea!" Chemi says. "Why don't you tell mine first?"

"Your wife doesn't know?"

There's no end to the revelations that stun Shuli. While he chews on that new bit of information, Chemi goes to the mini-fridge and pulls out two bottles of beer. He pops the tops and passes one to his guest. Turning his chair around, he straddles it, leaning over the back.

"She thinks I'm a programmer," Chemi says. "That I'm a freelancer. Which, in a way, I am. Why don't you break the news to her and we can see together if my life comes apart." At that, Chemi reaches across and clinks his bottle against Shuli's. A forced toast. "If you want to ruin all those other happy lives, you can write everyone on the list. Before you do, just be sure they'd rather have the truth than sleep at night."

What had this man already done to Shuli? And what an impossible position did he put him in now? The families must be told. But to tell them would only spread the agony of this terrible knowing.

Shuli suddenly feels so tired. A deep tired that makes him think he might actually sleep. He looks to that rickety cot.

"How far do you live from here?" Shuli asks.

"Not too far. Over by Ammunition Hill."

"Go home," Shuli says. "I need to think."

"You trust me to return?"

"No," Shuli says, "I don't. Why not leave me your driver's license and your *teudat zehut*?"

Chemi takes out his wallet and surrenders his license and his national identity card, in its cracked plastic sheath.

Chemi turns to go. As he steps away, Shuli grabs at his arm.

"Actually, take these," he says, giving back the IDs. "I'll take your phone instead. For those who move in the modern world, that's the most collateral one can give."

Chemi looks at his phone, contemplating, before handing it off.

"Is there a code?" Shuli says.

"No code. Just dial."

"And your home number?"

"Esther," Chemi says. "Pull up that name. That's my wife."

Shuli checks the contacts for the name. Satisfied, he aims the screen toward Chemi.

"Is Rav Katz's number in here?"

"You'll see it in the outgoing calls."

Shuli confirms this too, already dialing while Chemi is still there.

"It's a good idea," Chemi says, approving. "Talk to the rebbe. He's very wise."

XXVI

RAV KATZ STANDS AT THE EDGE OF THE BALCONY, A HAND thrust out toward his yeshiva—he'd come as soon as he'd heard. He wipes red-rimmed eyes against a shirtsleeve and turns to Shuli, leaning his weight against the railing. It creaks so loudly and lists so noticeably, Shuli is sure rabbi and rail will both go tumbling over.

"The room, right here, the whole time—hidden," Katz says. "Always, I felt like we had a guardian angel watching over us, and now to learn it's a monster peering in."

"Which is why we need to arrange for a *beis din,* so that he can be properly judged. It's preferable to the police, yes? This is a matter of Jewish law."

"I have a better idea. Why not call the newspapers and stick it on the front page?" Rav Katz twists at his beard, keeping a fist closed around it. "What good will come from dragging this ugliness into the courts? A story like this will spread until it reaches the Gentiles and embarrasses the Jews."

"You can't not want justice. Not after what you and I, what the students and all those poor people, have been subjected to.

A fraud. A con. He's a thief like any other and should be treated as such."

"Not like any other," Katz says. He frees his beard to light a cigarette, blowing a smoke ring Shuli's way. "A sin like his, one that reaches to Paradise, how could we find enough ways to punish him? Retribution is beyond us. It will only come when Leibovitch faces a Heavenly Tribunal."

If there were any room left for Shuli not to believe what he was hearing, he'd have added Katz's reply to the mix.

"You want to wait until he's dead of old age?" Shuli says.

"I didn't say that. I said he should face a Heavenly Tribunal. I wouldn't be surprised if that court came down from above to convene among the living. There's precedent for such manifestations. God has sent judges to this world before."

The rabbi ashes his cigarette over the edge of the railing and, as he turns to scan Jerusalem in the distance, Shuli's gaze follows.

"You're really not going to give me advice?"

"I'm the one who needs it," Katz says. "Where am I going to find an honest donor to make up for what, from this mamzer, will be missed?"

"At least help me figure out what to tell the victims. I've been learning at your yeshiva, which means I'm your student. You can't just leave me to fend for myself."

"Whoever asked you to show up at my doorstep? Charity toward you doesn't make me your keeper."

"Please!" Shuli begs, pressing his hands together.

"You do what you need, but not with my blessing."

Rav Katz takes one last glance over the edge of the balcony

before ducking out through the metal door to the landing. Shuli latches it closed behind him. Every footfall of the rebbe's can be heard as he hurries down the stairs.

Exhausted beyond reason, Shuli practically crawls into the apartment and lies down on the cot, pulling the pillow over his eyes.

WHEN SHULI OPENS HIS EYES AGAIN, HE FINDS HIMSELF IN darkness. He's at first unsure where he is. He then remembers he's in Jerusalem, in evil Chemi's hut of an apartment, and is overcome with joy that he has his *kinyan* back, and then with sadness because everything else has gone abominably wrong.

Sitting up, placing his feet firmly on the floor, he senses that it's both floor and not floor, and—giving his toes a wiggle—concludes that he's both awake and still dreaming. Looking around, now somehow seeing without light, he understands that he's back in a place he'd been before.

Shuli presses himself to standing and double-checks his purchase in this otherworldly world. Finding himself steady, he turns on a lamp out of habit and then strips off his clothes. He goes into that narrow bathroom to take a shower, and as he washes himself, he notices beside it a deep pool. When he is clean as clean can be, down to his nails, Shuli jumps into the pool, dunking himself deep. Remembering his wedding ring, he pops up and slides the ring off to avoid *chatzitzah*. Submerged again, he feels, in this *mikvah*, pure.

Considering the pool's sudden appearance where it couldn't possibly be, Shuli isn't at all surprised when he steps out into the room in a towel and sees an ornate cupboard, so much like the ark that holds the Torah at the yeshiva.

Opening it, he finds a pristine *kittel* on a hanger. Shuli takes down the robe, starched and fresh, a brilliant white. He fastens the snaps, and it fits him nicely, reaching down to his calves. The robe is not markedly unlike the one he himself wears on the High Holidays, and in which he will one day be buried.

As he makes his way further into the dream, stepping out onto the balcony, Shuli stands where Rav Katz had and stares up at a sky, blacker than black, the stars particularly aglow. Shuli marvels at how magical is the universe and how unnaturally bright the night. Shuli thinks again that, yes, he's in a dream.

Stepping through the metal door and out onto the landing, he crosses directly through the door opposite, where usually there was a solid wall. He knows this door can't have been there. But hadn't it felt the same when he'd first sought the entrance to Chemi's? Maybe this one too had always been there, but he'd likewise paid it no mind when climbing up and down between the yeshiva and the street above.

The balcony on which he finds himself is the same as Chemi's. But right where the apartment would be is a grand and complicated house. Isn't this just the way things were in Nachlaot! Hadn't Shuli always said that about this neighborhood? One really never could tell what wonders lurked behind a gate.

Shuli lets himself in to find that the structure is even larger inside than it appears from without. He roams a maze of hallways, and Shuli knows just when to turn and when to go straight, when to climb or descend a staircase. He glides along this way, floating as one might on an inner tube in a river, until he reaches the mouth of the dream.

Because of the *mikvah,* and the white *kittel* he'd been gifted to wear on his journey, Shuli presumes that, when he turns the knob on the imposing door in front of him, when he steps into the room on the other side, he'll find the Heavenly Tribunal of which Rav Katz had told him. This must be the *Beit Din Shamayim* come down from the upper reaches, to receive his testimony against Chemi.

Though he can't still his trembling legs, Shuli does his best to straighten himself to his full height and barrels into the room.

To his great disappointment, there are no judges waiting, and, looking up, no celestial gallery of kaddish.com souls watching over the proceedings.

Only one of those Chemi has wronged is there. Shuli is relieved to find his stiff-armed father, with his hands stuck out, perched on a high stool. Shuli is not at all stunned to discover his own elbows gone as well.

His father smiles warmly, looking more angelic and divine than he had in the other dream. This makes Shuli happy, for his father is so deserving, and sad because it is so clearly a characteristic of the dead.

His father also wears the *kittel,* with its broad sleeves and flowing skirt, the white sash cinched tightly around his waist. It's the exact robe his father had worn to their family seders, complete with the crimson stains from Passovers of yore. This reminds Shuli of food, and he looks behind him to see if the feast has returned. There's nothing there, and with the conspicuous absence of food and drink, and with both of them dressed in white, yes, maybe it is Yom Kippur, the Day of Atonement.

As a greeting, Shuli says to his father, "I miss you so much," and "I wish you'd gotten to meet my children, they're very good children," and "How lovely to see you today, looking so . . . rested."

"Today? But there are no days here," his father says, in his old voice, with his old mouth, and his old normal tongue set in its normal place.

It's so good to hear his father talk, instead of making that terrible birdlike sound, that Shuli cries. "I'm just happy to be together," Shuli says. "And I was worried it was Yom Kippur."

"There's no reason to worry. It's nice to atone. If no one from the living ever advocated for you, it's a comfort to take action in cleansing the soul. What's wrong with a fast without end?"

"Without end" he hadn't said. Shuli feels his legs go weaker. He looks for a place to sit but there's only the stool his father uses.

Rushing for the closest wall against which to steady himself, Shuli tries to look cheery, grinning like a fool. Yes, yes, how nice for you! How nice that you have purpose, that you have a reason to not-live!

"Abba, is it really like this, for always, the fasting? No feast, even with the straightened arms?"

His father tells him that it is like this, unceasing, and then looks down at his elbowless arms with some trepidation, as if he hadn't noticed that part before.

What Shuli can't understand is how such conditions were possible.

One earthly year—what they'd always been taught, what he himself said to his students. This was the maximum period a soul might be purged in the afterlife. And yet, twenty years later, here his father is caught in a ceaseless kind of *kaparah*.

"Eleven months of Kaddish. One year of judgment," Shuli begins reeling off halachah. "This—it's against the rules!"

His father waves away such irrelevant lower-world notions. Without elbows, the swing of that arm, the billowing *kittel* sleeve, it's as painful to look upon as that darting, spear-like tongue.

"A year is still the maximum," his father says. "Only without day and without night to signify change, without a son who has been studiously saying Kaddish to go silent at the eleventh month, how are we to know when judgment comes to an end without such markers?"

Shuli, already sweating, says, "I will fix it, Abba. Don't worry. For you, and for all the others. I will put it right."

"You will?" his father says, looking oh so happy. "For all of us? For all the twenty-eight hundred? The hunger, it does admittedly wear."

"I will. I promise. For all two thousand seven hundred and ninety-four."

Hearing that, his father curls forward on the stool and masks his face with the draping sleeves of his outstretched arms. It's not out of sadness, Shuli can tell, but a flush of fatherly pride. His son, finally doing what's right.

With his father leaning forward, a new door is revealed. It had been hidden behind his flowing robe when he'd been sitting erect.

Shuli dares not interrupt this moment of relief. He steps to his father's side and reaches for the knob, slipping by.

Upon entering, Shuli is immediately confused, for the next room is the same as the last. There's still no feast. There's still one stool. And, atop it, his father, as Shuli had just left him, with his face pressed into his arms and those arms jutting out like stilts.

When this new father hears him close the door, he sits up, revealing his face. Shuli is shocked to see not his father but his sister perched there, and to find that her robe has the same stains. Pinned to Dina's hair is the identical black velvet yarmulke that their father had always worn. And the modest *peot* by her ears are a pair of tight curls fallen loose, Dina's hair tied back.

His sister stares at Shuli and Shuli stares at her. To see Dina dressed exactly as their father, to see her dressed exactly as a man, unsettles. She's always been so faithful, so Orthodox and restrained. She is in no way a seeker of egalitarianism or reform.

"Sister!" he says, full of love. What a comfort to find her in this cold place.

She motions him closer with that same horrible wave, her sleeve sliding back as her arm windmills around. Shuli can't help but notice the leather strap of tefillin wrapped around his sister's hand and running up that unbending arm.

Looking back to her face, he sees the black box resting on her head, and the two straps from the *shel rosh* running down the front of the garment, black against white.

He approaches, as instructed, and Dina—not at all disparaging—says, "I can't tell if the surprise on your face is from finding me here or from the tefillin I wear."

"It's not like you, sister," Shuli says.

"Isn't it?" Shuli's expression clearly says he doesn't think so. "Well, no matter. Rashi's daughters were already wearing tefillin in medieval times."

"But, sister, don't you remember our fight over the Kaddish? In the past, you've been resistant to adopting the ways of men."

His sister laughs and laughs, so that the stool rocks on uneven feet.

"Seriously, Larry? What are the ways of men? It doesn't even make sense. Why would there ever be a difference among the practices of Jews?"

Shuli is thrilled to see her in such fine form. He feels so loving, so happy, he asks if it would be all right, arms and all, if he gave her a hug.

"Oh, how I'd have enjoyed that, my Larry," she says. "But here I am pure, as in the times of the *Beit HaMikdash,* when the Holy Temple stood. And you, my brother, are as yet *tamei*—tainted by your transgressions. Still, I want you to know, you and I are good, brother. Fixing things between yourself and our father fixes them with me. It's other accounts that need settling."

"Do you mean with Miri?" he asks.

This she doesn't dignify with an answer.

It was the fish, he knew. Their puckered mouths. Their fierce, dumb hunger. It was the fish feasting and the defilement of his sister's home.

"Is it about your house?"

"A home has no feelings, Larry. That's your guess? Always shortcuts with you. Always, with emotion, you take the easy way out."

"Whatever it is, I'll fix it for you," he says. And reading his sister's face, the familiar roll of her eyes, Shuli tries again. "I mean," he says, "I'll fix it for myself."

Shuli walks around Dina to where he knows another door must stand, obscured. Finding it, he turns that handle and pushes through. He crosses the threshold with his eyes pressed shut, squeezing them tight in the dream, so that he may open them on the other side, in the waking world, so that he may discover himself flat out in Chemi's cot, eager to do what must be done.

He'd committed to his father.

He'd taken a pledge before his sister.

Opening his eyes, Shuli unleashes a howl that echoes around that same empty room, no different from the one right before and the one again before that, aside from a peculiar shimmering light in the edges of his vision, a sort of blanching glare bouncing up from the floor.

Seeking wisdom, he looks to where his father sat and his sister sat, but there's no one, and nothing there, not even the stool. He can see right to the door on the other side, poised outside the glare. Shuli's sure that the cot, that his sleeping self, must lie right beyond.

He hurries for the exit, only to bump into the back of a deep downy chair, with a large downy pillow, fluffed as if for the seder, as if Shuli was meant to drop down, in his holiday *kittel,* and recline.

Shuli goes around and melts into the chair, so unsteady are his legs, and so great is his exhaustion—which has returned with a vengeance. Seated, the light shines more brightly, nearly blinding. But that's nothing next to the chair's comfort, and the sharp contrast of all that physical weight lifted against all the personal pain he shoulders.

From his new vantage, Shuli makes out a table in front of him, the source of all that brilliance. He sinks deeper into the chair, so that he might prop his tired feet up on the table's edge. And there it is, a sea of glass set atop it. Not the light's source, but what catches and reflects it, kicking it back Shuli's way and making for that curious shimmer.

As his eyes continue to adapt, Shuli can make out more and more, and is startled to see a pair of feet on the other side of that round table, propped up on the edge, like his. A mirror.

The more he stares, the more the brightness dims, and the feet, smaller and narrower, appear to be a woman's. Raising his gaze, Shuli can see that it is indeed a woman, in a chair identical to Shuli's, sitting across. She, like his sister, and like his father, is wearing the white *kittel*. But on her, it is wide open, the sash undone.

He does not recognize her face. And does not know if it's rude in this place to ask her who she is. Was it possible, as the third person to appear, that she's the last of the Heavenly Tribunal? That maybe this is indeed his chance to take witness, and the reason he'd finally—so weary—been offered a chair? Shuli races through all his learning, trying to decide if he'd ever read of a tribunal where the three judges weren't seated in a row.

Shuli concentrates on this question while struggling to recognize that face and fighting to keep his gaze away from the body, naked beneath that open robe.

"Who are you?" he says.

The woman makes no move to answer.

And Shuli, failing to resist, looks to the woman's breasts and to her belly and then right between her spread legs.

Shuli does not know who she is, until he does.

How disgraceful! The face he couldn't recall, but now, looking down . . . Sitting across is the woman who had once looked out at him (without seeing), who had performed for Shuli (without knowing) using that giant glass dildo.

With her own elbowless arms, she motions to the table, sort of waving a hand above, so that he might focus on the array between them.

The table is set with a rich assortment of blown glass. Dildos of differing heights, with differing tapers to their rounded tips. It's a beautiful and well-crafted selection with which one might pleasure oneself.

Without the years separating them, and without the shield of his religious transformation, without the ether of the Internet and the anonymity of his one-sided screen-fed view, Shuli can't bear to sit before her, himself appraised.

Shuli looks to the door in the wall, through which he might escape. But this time, when he looks, there's no door there. He does not turn around, knowing what's already happened to the one behind.

This room, this was it. It was just as his father had taught him. For some maybe it was Heaven, but for Shuli, boxed in, it was Hell. Here he was facing this woman, shamed for what could be all of interminable time.

Shuli turns to her as she reaches, with her rigid, unyielding arms, to the table.

With great control, and great delicacy, she takes up a spiral, glass dildo, containing all the colors of the rainbow. Smiling, signaling, Reb Shuli knows, as with so many things in that sphere, that she means for him to lean back and away.

Yes, it was like Passover, as he'd assumed. Shuli sighs and relaxes; he leans into that deep cloud of a pillow on his chair. This lowers the trunk of his body, bringing his torso forward, so that, with his feet pressed to the table's edge, his knees bend further, rising higher than before.

He does not quite comprehend what she's now asking. With the limited mobility in her arms, it's more difficult for her to cue the pulling up of his robe. When he grasps what she wants, he raises the *kittel*'s skirt, tugging it open along the snaps, and the woman leans forward, reaching toward him.

But the parts? Shuli's parts? Still, he scooches further and does what he thinks he's being told.

And, do you believe it? With the robe unfastened, when looking down between his legs, Shuli sees that—though he'd always known himself to be a man—he's also a woman too.

Shifting this way, and shifting that, he makes room in himself to receive the kindness the woman across now offers.

And feeling himself full up, the wand brimming him, there's a wonderful sort of tightness and a wonderful sort of pressure, and a sensation in places of himself that he—or "she," Shuli thinks, possibly she—hadn't previously known might be excited.

So relieved is Shuli, so pleasured and stimulated is Shuli, so transformed is Shuli by this back-and-forth, sea-like rocking inside, that Shuli only wants to return to this woman the peace and pleasure that she gives.

Tipping his torso forward so that Shuli might reach with those rigid arms, Shuli takes up from the table an instrument of appropriate height and appropriate gauge, offering what Shuli hopes might be just the right amount of comfort.

And as she had inserted in Shuli, Shuli—meeting her gaze, marking her approval—inserts into her. It's an act that only increases the rewarding fullness Shuli feels within.

As Shuli's eyes turn heavy and slowly close, weighted as

they are in delight, Shuli can see that the woman, her good turn requited, is also on the way to sleep.

In this way, maintaining a rhythm, and in this way, gliding back and forth, Shuli finally understands what it is to find one's place in Paradise.

XXVII

I T'S THE MIDDLE OF THE DAY WHEN SHULI WAKES. HE KNOWS if he's to achieve what he'd pledged in his sleep, he'll need to move with great speed. He also knows that before he attends to ethereal matters, there's an earthly debt of gratitude still to be repaid.

Shuli rushes straight from Chemi's apartment to Mea Shearim, to the street where the silversmiths ply their wares.

He has no idea which shop is best, or which artisan has more talent than any other. He can't tell anything from peering at the window displays—aesthetics is not where Shuli shines. In the end, he settles on the store with the biggest sign in English.

The woman behind the counter leaves Shuli to browse. But Shuli doesn't want to be left alone. He wants advice. He catches her attention and sees that her eyes, like his, look tired in a way that no rest would ever erase. She offers him a businesslike smile and Shuli smiles back at her, twice as hard.

"Can I help you?" she asks, addressing him in English from the start.

"Do you ship to America? I want to send something there."

"That's what you're looking for? Good shipping?" she says, tucking a loose lock of hair back into her snood. "That's your big concern, before you buy your soon-to-be daughter-in-law her wedding silver?"

"There's no daughter-in-law in the works," Shuli says. "And for me, yes, shipping to America is, my apologies, the number one concern."

"Our business is shipping to America. It's our specialty," she says, planting her elbows on the counter. "You name it, we pack it up good and ship it out. Big and small. Any value." Straightening up, she calls through the archway behind her, to what appears to be a backroom workshop. "Tell him! Do we pack it up good, Shmulik?"

"We pack it the best," Shmulik yells in return.

"We insure it here," she says. "And on the customs form, we put 'zero dollars.' No trouble on either end. You don't worry. It'll get there, and get there unbroken and unstolen. Not a dent either. *Chick-chock*, they'll have it. Two days, even, if you want to pay for the DHL."

"Good," Reb Shuli says. "Excellent." He looks around at the treasures in the room, scanning the shelves. "I need something special."

"Special is our other specialty," the woman says, again tucking at the same lock of hair that keeps escaping from the bottom of her snood. "Do you see anything you like?"

Shuli makes a quick show of perusing candlesticks and mezuzot, silver trays and Torah crowns.

"I don't see exactly what I need."

The woman again yells to the back, calling for Shmulik, who trudges out in a heavy apron, looking like he's been working in a mine. "This one wants special," she says, pulling at the apron's bib and bringing Shmulik right up to the edge of the counter. From the way she speaks, and the way she pulls, Shuli assumes he is her husband.

To Shuli she says, "This is the silversmith. He makes everything here."

Shmulik the silversmith pokes around in a display case, hunting for something, and then, giving up, wipes his hands on the apron, fronts and backs. There is no discernible change in their cleanliness as far as Shuli can tell.

"You looking for custom work?" the man says.

"Maybe," Shuli says. "I think so. I'm after a Kiddush cup. Something to stop the breath."

"And you don't see it out?"

Shuli stands quiet.

"You think I'm sensitive? I'm here to work. Show me something close to what you want and we'll go from there."

"Can you put things on it?"

"Like images?" he asks. "The cluster of grapes? A pomegranate?"

"Like words," Shuli says.

Here the woman waves a hand as if to say, *katan alav,* that there is no challenge the silversmith can't meet. She does this with a flourish, with the ease the bent-elbowed have at their disposal.

"You want him to engrave?" she says. "He'll engrave. You want raised? Bas-relief, high relief—you know, high relief?—he'll do anything you want. Once, for a customer in Tzfat, he carved the whole text of the *Pirkei Avot* into a small silver egg. It took a magnifying glass to read it. Every letter, perfect."

"I want big," Shuli says.

"With letters, big is easier than little," she says. "That's the point. If he can do the egg, he can do the cup."

Shuli again surveys their wares, overwhelmed. And the woman, a good salesperson, says, "Take your time," and returns to her work. The silversmith remains at her side staring at Shuli, but after she gives him a shove, he studies the floor.

Finally, Shuli spots a chalice sitting on a high shelf. "I want like that," Shuli says.

"That?" she says.

"That?" the silversmith says.

"What's wrong with that?" Shuli wants to know.

"That one's not for Kiddush," the woman tells him. "That's for Pesach. That's a *cos Eliyahu*," she says of the oversize goblet, in which wine is poured for the prophet Elijah during seder.

She drags a stool over to the wall and, climbing up, retrieves it for him. Before handing it over, she rotates it so Shuli might see the intricate filigree that was its centerpiece. It did indeed read *"Cos Eliyahu"* in large Hebrew letters.

"Yes," Shuli says, undaunted, and measuring its heft. "I want like this, but for *Shabbos*."

"You want a Pesach cup for regular *Shabbos*?" the silversmith says.

"No, I want a Kiddush cup. But big like that. Where it says *'Cos Eliyahu,'* in the middle, I want it to say *'Cos Gavriel.'*"

"You want a cup for the angel Gavriel?" the woman says.

"More or less," Shuli says, admiring the one he holds. Looking up, he says, "It's for my friend."

The way they gawk at him in return, Shuli feels he should explain. "A friend that's a child," he says. "A present for a boy going through a rough time. I want the name nice and big. Something you can read from across the room."

"Sure," the silversmith says. "Not a problem." And he turns to the woman that Shuli is now sure is his wife.

"Not a problem," she says. "When do you need it?"

"As soon as possible."

"A week," the silversmith says, without hesitation.

"You sure, Shmulik?" the woman asks, giving him the eye. When he makes clear that he is, she says to Shuli, "Done. A week."

"If you can do the shipping—"

"We are known for the shipping. I already said, our strength!" Then she raises an eyebrow and tucks at that hair. "Don't you want to know what it costs? That cup you hold is a real *beheimah*. That's a lot of silver."

"Whatever it is, it is."

The woman takes the *cos Eliyahu* back and, tipping it over, she shows Shuli the price tag taped into the curve of its base. "That's for this one," she says, and Shuli can tell she wants him to look stunned. When he doesn't, she turns to the silversmith. "How much extra for custom?"

The man looks at the price on the cup and then sizes up Shuli.

"I'll do it for the same. No extra." And, looking proud, he says, "I'll make something special for your friend."

The woman produces an order form and begins to fill it out. The silversmith recedes into his workroom, and almost immediately Shuli hears the sound of an engine's whir.

"Where's it going?" the woman asks.

Shuli gives her Gavriel's name and the address of the school.

"Do you want a gift card?"

"No," Shuli says. "He'll know who it's from. Just send it to the school, at his attention. That's all."

"A lucky boy," she says. "Is it his bar mitzvah?"

"Soon," Shuli says.

The woman reaches under the counter and produces a credit card machine.

"Cash," Shuli says, and takes out his envelope, with the money he'd planned to return to Miri, to show how carefully he'd saved. "Are dollars OK?"

"Cash is always OK. You want to do euros? You want to do pounds? I'll take rupees if you've got them. Money is money."

Shuli empties his envelope and hands it to the woman. She counts it out. He's three hundred dollars short.

"Would you trust a man to pay it off?" Shuli says.

The sound of the machine's engine stops. Shuli is amazed that the silversmith even heard.

"We don't do that," Shmulik calls from the back.

"This isn't a car dealership," the woman says. "There are no payment plans."

"It's silver," the silversmith yells.

"He's right," the woman says. "The object is money itself. *Kesef zeh kesef,*" she says in Hebrew, which is the same as her "money is money" but now with a different intent. She does not like his plan. "Why not put it on a card?"

"It's complicated," he says. "A moment of transition. But you can trust me to pay."

The woman taps the counter with her pen, considering. Shuli, self-conscious, looks around the shop at the smaller Kiddush cups and all the tiny silver thimbles, the kind that one might send to a newborn child. When he meets her gaze, she shakes her head, as if disappointed with herself.

"Six months," she says. "Six payments."

"Hadas!" the man calls from the back, for the first time using the woman's name.

"You get back to working," she yells to him. "I'll worry about who gets paid."

Again the machine in the backroom hums.

"Don't make me a fool in front of this one," she says to Shuli, tilting her head toward the archway and the silversmith beyond. "Honestly, it's not worth it if I have to hear about you for the rest of my life."

"I will pay," Shuli says. "Debts, in this world, I no longer let sit."

XXVIII

TOWARD REPAYING THOSE DEBTS, SHULI SETS TO WORK as soon as he's back at Chemi's apartment. He breaks only to put on tefillin and say *Minchah* and *Maariv* down at the yeshiva, praying along with the students and Rav Katz, who—a man of great heart—welcomes Shuli even now.

When they sing *Aleinu*, Shuli grabs his knapsack and duffel and ducks out, dashing back to the files. He starts right in on a new name, reading the application, memorizing personal information, and reviewing each page with real *kavanah*. So focused is Shuli, it's well after midnight when he next notices the time.

He rubs at his eyes. He stretches and sighs his way through a creaky deep-knee bend. And then he appraises what he'd already accomplished. At this point there's no denying it. Like Nachshon at the Red Sea, Shuli thinks he's waded far enough into the waters to show he means business.

Fetching Chemi's phone, he steps out to pace nervously on the balcony and dials Miri.

Shuli knows he's been lax in reaching out during the madness of the last days and Miri, rightfully, sits silent on the other end when she hears his voice. Without prompt or cue, he slowly and carefully fills her in, explaining how he'd found Chemi and reclaimed his rights, how he'd uncovered the hoax and then dreamt his edifying dream.

Shuli winces as he waits on her reply. What Miri says, tender and serene, is, "What of us, Shuli? When will you make your way home?"

He couldn't ask for more.

Loving wife. Understanding wife. He feels, by her companionship, lifted up and blessed. "It's not about returning to a specific place," Shuli says. "It's about us being together. What if you three were to join me to build a new home here."

"There?" she says. "In Israel?"

"In Jerusalem," he says. "The Holy City."

"You really have gone mad," she says. "Our life is in Brooklyn. Our house is in Brooklyn. What would we even do over there—how would the family survive?"

"By God's grace," he says. "And, because grace won't feed us, I have, for that too, a plan."

"Is that supposed to calm me? Your plans unravel, Shuli. Your plans unwind."

But this plan had unwound its way to Jerusalem. And as much as Miri has Shuli's number, he knows a thing or two about her. He knows how deep her faith runs, and how strong within it is the desire to live in the earthly city that mirrors the one in Heaven.

"We can have a great life here," Shuli says. "I've already seen our future, pictured our new beginning."

"Now you're a seer? I'd rather be married to a wise man than a prophet," Miri says, borrowing a line from *Bava Batra*.

"Wisdom I can try for too. If you want logic, if you want proof," and Shuli looks down on the yeshiva's dome, and thinks of all his collected learning. "The *chachamim* say that to live in *Eretz Yisrael* is equal to doing all the other *mitzvot* of the Torah combined. And the Ramban makes clear, to live as we do in America, it's as if one is worshipping idols."

"Now we're all sinners? Every one of us, faithful from afar?"

"I did not say 'sinner,' God forbid. I said only that the Ramban writes '*k'ilu*'—that it is 'as *if*' one were living that way."

"And that's why you want your children to join you? To spare them from sin?"

"I want them here because I miss them and can't live without them—and because I miss you," Shuli says. "Because I love you, and love the children, and because I've found a way to take all this terrible deception and turn it back into truth."

"Please!" Miri says, her patience gone. "Enough already! You got your *kinyan*, you got your rights. You can't go on this way, shoveling things into an emptiness that never gets filled."

"No, no," Shuli says, "a misunderstanding." He actually laughs out loud, feeling lighthearted. "It's not about me anymore—that's the wonder. It's the others, less fortunate, that I'm here to serve."

There is a worrying silence. He presses the phone to his ear and can hear a siren on Miri's end and the raucous sounds of Hayim and Nava at play.

When she finally speaks, Miri says, "So you're whole now, my husband?"

"Like never before. Except in my love for you, and in my fatherly pride, where there's never been, for even a moment, any doubt."

Shuli holds his breath and thinks he might explode with delight when Miri says, "I've always imagined what it would be like for our children to live in the Holy City."

"Then you'll think about it?"

"Yes, my husband, I'll think."

Miracles atop miracles. How quickly a life can turn around.

INVIGORATED, SHULI POKES THROUGH THE FILES, HIS ATTEN-tion never lagging. He never feels tired during his inquiry, and is bothered by neither hunger nor thirst. By the time the sun rises, Shuli has a partial list committed to memory, and a physical pile to make it manifest. When he shuts his eyes, the names slowly come.

Shuli decides he's sufficiently well versed in the first thirteen— not just in his command of the names but with the essence of the people behind them. A baker's dozen under his belt. And a not-unlucky number where Jews are concerned.

As Shuli finalizes that first solid stack of files, he thinks he might manage to finish another that day if his memory holds out. Before moving on, he texts Chemi's wife, saying only, "Tell your husband his friend Shuli found his phone and would like to return it." Shuli thinks that'll do the trick, and waits for Chemi to come back.

As concerns Chemi's wife, let him find his own way to honesty and amends.

When Chemi arrives, Shuli is at the railing reciting his list aloud and checking it against the sheet of paper where he'd written it. To hold a full hundred in his head, he'd need a while longer, that was certain.

"Six people," Shuli says to Chemi. "Six a year. And on some, seven."

"Six a year, what?"

"New customers. At a new, fairer rate. If you give me the passwords and show me how to do the site," Shuli says. "So I can make it real. So I can make the money and also pray. I've done the math. I know the numbers. If my wife will come and teach. And if I teach some. Plus, with our house in Royal Hills. If we flip it, we should be all right."

Shuli leads Chemi into the apartment and shows him the shifting drifts of papers, the freshly organized piles, pointing him to the stack set apart.

"There will be ninety-four in that one when it's done," Shuli says. "Ninety-four seems best, for the first year, to start."

Chemi opens the top folder. "This one is very old. One of the first."

"Yes," Shuli says. "I'm doing my best to maintain a kind of order. That is, the ones still under Divine judgment will, of course, go first. And then the very oldest will go, along with the newest. That makes the most sense."

"Who does it make sense for?"

"For me. And for you. And for the families. And for the dead," Shuli says. "I'll pray. I'll say every Kaddish missed, for every soul forgotten. If I do ninety-four this year, and take on six new customers, paying—that makes a hundred. A hundred names a year to start."

"Then it would take—" Chemi stares off, starting to tally in his head.

"Thirty years," Shuli says. "At a hundred a year, thirty years to put things right. I'll be eighty then. A nice number!"

Shuli shifts his weight nervously from foot to foot, as if he were interviewing for the job. As if the two, in cahoots, were working on a deal.

To further plead his case, Shuli says, "In such an instance, it's absolutely not a sin to say Kaddish for more than one person at a time."

While Chemi processes, a pained expression on his face, Shuli goes over it for himself once again. As long as he goes through each name, each time, in his prayers. As long as his thoughts are with the dead, individually, in each instance, against this part of the process he can think of no prohibition.

As for those for whom the prayers come so very late, a merciful God must surely consider extenuating circumstances now and again. And anyway, back to Shuli's dream, and his fasting father, what is it to be late by a few years when set against an eternity? In the everlastingness of Heaven, with infinity stretching as far back before the beginning as it does out into the future past the end, a mourning delayed by even a thousand, thousand years is nothing but a blink against time.

"I'd thought it would be over with, this torment," Chemi says. "But this—"

"Yes," Shuli says, speaking with something like compassion. "I imagine it's a bit of a shock."

Chemi scratches at his nose, aghast.

"Come now, don't look so sad," Shuli says. "Would prison really be better? You paying with yourself for what you can't in any other way repay? This is a much more attractive offer. For you, for your wife, for your kids—you said you had kids, yes?"

"Five," Chemi says. "There are five."

"How much better for them! And the sooner you help me

start chipping away at it, the sooner this will all be forgotten. The first twenty years went by so fast. Think of how quick the next thirty can be."

"Yes," Chemi says, reaching for a different file.

"The passwords," Shuli says. "I don't mean to rush you. But there are still many names for me to practice, and they'll be starting *Shacharit* soon."

Chemi leads Shuli to the crate with the router and pulls a little notebook out from underneath the device. "Everything's in here. The bank numbers, the passwords, all that you need."

Shuli takes it and extends a hand, which Chemi shakes.

Then Chemi turns away with the face of a man whose life has just been burdened out into the future. As he walks off, he drops the keys onto the table and picks up his phone. "Rav Katz has the number," he says, and steps out onto the balcony and through the metal door.

Shuli watches him go. He then heads right to one of the piles and pores over a daughter's reminiscences about a mother who was said to extract true joy from the small things in life.

How long until he could hold a hundred people in his thoughts while he prayed?

Shuli doesn't let the worry slow him. He pushes toward the practical and the positive in his mind.

If they get a good price on the Royal Hills house? If Rav Katz helps him find some teaching in the neighborhood? He seems to like Shuli's style.

Shuli will figure it out. He'll remember the names. And when Miri comes around—he knows she will—Shuli can make room for the family right where he is. That balcony could be enclosed. A tin roof and some cinder block. He and Miri could live in the addition while the children sleep within. They could take their time finding an apartment to fit.

Shuli puts down the papers and grabs his tallis bag from Nava's knapsack and the keys from the table, and, as if he's been doing it forever, he locks the apartment, and the door to the stairs, as he heads to the study hall for minyan.

Gilad is already waiting, and Shuli takes his place across from the boy. He puts on his tallis and wraps his tefillin, and then they both turn eastward toward the Temple Mount.

Shuli moves through the blessings, rote and second nature, practicing instead the names on his list. He can do it, he knows. He can take on a hundred lives each year. He can keep them in his thoughts, and learn to daven at the same time with a whole heart. Shuli believes this more and more as each second passes by.

And when the first Kaddish comes, Shuli takes to his feet.

Acknowledgments

I want to thank my editor, Jordan Pavlin, and my agent, Nicole Aragi, for getting me, and the novel, to this point. I wouldn't be here without either of them, very literally. I want to thank Jordan Rodman, Gracie Dietshe, and Nicholas Thomson, and all the amazing folk at Knopf and Team Aragi. I'm indebted to Deborah Landau and NYU for their continued support, and to John Wray for my hideout. I've turned to many friends with fact-related questions, often hyper-specific and wholly neurotic. JJ fielded the sunflower seeds, David H2 tackled Memphis, my brother-in-law counted Kaddishes, and on and on. Joel Weiss was an extraordinary resource and counsel, as always. Chris Adrian read the manuscript early. And Merle Englander never fails to catch a typo before we go to press. As for Lauren Holmes, there are no words—it defies dedication. But I'll go with thank you, thank you for your support. And to my wife, Rachel, and my daughter, Olivia, there is thanks, and there is love.

Nathan Englander is the author of the story collections *For the Relief of Unbearable Urges,* an international best seller, and *What We Talk About When We Talk About Anne Frank,* and the novels *The Ministry of Special Cases* and *Dinner at the Center of the Earth.* His books have been translated into twenty-two languages. He is the recipient of a Guggenheim Fellowship, a PEN/Malamud Award, the Frank O'Connor International Short Story Award, and the Sue Kaufman Prize from the American Academy of Arts and Letters, and was a finalist for the Pulitzer Prize in 2013. His play, *The Twenty-Seventh Man,* premiered at the Public Theater in 2012. He is Distinguished Writer in Residence at New York University and lives in Brooklyn, New York, with his wife and daughter.

Pierre Simon Fournier *le jeune* (1712–1768), who designed the type used in this book, was both an originator and a collector of types. His services to the art of printing were his design of letters, his creation of ornaments and initials, and his standardization of type sizes. His types are old style in character and sharply cut. In 1764 and 1766 he published his *Manuel typographique,* a treatise on the history of French types and printing, on typefounding in all its details, and on what many consider his most important contribution to typography—the measurement of type by the point system.

Typeset by Scribe, Philadelphia, Pennsylvania

Printed and bound by Berryville Graphics, Berryville, Virginia

Designed by Betty Lew